Christmas in CHESHIRE BAY

USA TODAY BESTSELLING AUTHOR

H.M. SHANDER

Lynne &
Carol

happy holidays.

Shander

Christmas in Cheshire Bay

Published by H.M. Shander Publishing
Copyright 2022 H.M. Shander

Cover Design: Eleanor Lloyd-Jones @ Shower of Schmidt Designs
Editing: PWA & IDIM Editorial
Shander, H.M., 1975—Christmas in Cheshire Bay

Dedicated to a summer of broken dreams,
afternoons spent in the backyard
under the red umbrella with an iced coffee in hand.
And to the Squirrels — Duncan & Carlos and their kids,
Cedar, George & Rusty

Table of Contents

Chapter One

udio books were my favourite, and I could listen to them for hours, if the narrator was any good. However, the book playing over the speakers of my car was terrible, the voice grating yet monotone. It was supposed to be a fairy-tale retelling but instead of hoping the proverbial damsel in distress would be rescued by the supposed hero, I found myself wishing he'd run in the opposite direction as far away from her as possible.

Doing the same, I ejected the CD with a huff, tossing *Cassidy's Cryptic Cauldron* onto the passenger seat, but the disc missed and hit the floorboard instead.

"Oh, for crying out loud." I groaned and gripped the wheel as I bent over the consul.

The highway was deserted, so I took my eyes off the road for a split second and stretched out my arm until the edge of my fingertips touched the CD. Slowly I inched it toward me and grabbed it firmly, putting it back on the seat.

Correcting myself as I had drifted just over the centre line, I yanked the wheel hard to the right. Suddenly, a boom came from the front passenger side and the car tipped on the forward edge.

"Shit!"

I gripped the wheel with all my strength and stabbed the hazard lights button on my dash, nearly chipping a manicured fingernail. The car was heavy and difficult to control all the while the strangest sound circled around me.

My best guess? I blew a tire.

Slowly, shoulders scrunched up against my neck trying to drown out the awful sound, I drove the car over to the side of the road and put it into park.

I took a sip of my still-warm cinnamon-scented latte and reached into the back seat for my hat and mitts before I killed the engine.

Thrusting my fake-fur lined gloves on, I stepped onto the vacant road and walked over to the passenger side, staring at what was left of the shredded tire with a heavy sigh.

"Well, that's bloody fantastic." I tossed my hands into the air and let out an ear-piercing scream into the void of snow-covered, coniferous trees.

I was still a good thirty minutes outside of Cheshire Bay, and that was the nearest town.

The universe continued to rain down its parade of nastiness. If it wasn't one thing going wrong over this blessed holiday, it was nine other things. Why couldn't it be January already? Nothing major in my life ever went wrong in January. It was often too cold.

I opened the trunk and lifted the lid where underneath sat the spare. Never in my whole life had I changed a tire – I had no idea how that even worked, but youTube would have a video. However, as I scrolled, each video was in excess of twenty minutes, and my rapidly draining phone in the sub-zero temperatures didn't have that kind of battery.

I should've stayed home. Made up some wild excuse to convince my sister I wasn't making the drive, sent a sizable cheque to excuse my absence, and called it a day. That would've been better than making the painful drive to a place I swore I'd never want to see again. Instead, I'm stranded on the side of the highway, in the middle of nowhere, a good half hour drive from her place.

From our family's summer home.

The one Mom died in fourteen years ago.

As anger at being delayed with another unexpected issue boiled, I dialled Lily's number after climbing back into my cooling down car.

My younger sister picked up on the first ring. "Hey, Mona."

"Hey, Lil. I'm going to be late."

Majorly late.

"You're not coming, are you?" My little sister's voice fell in a self-defeating way.

My breath was visible in the glow from my phone, and I

swore the dampness was freezing into miniature crystals.

"Of course, I am." The need to chastise her on the tip of my tongue, but I closed my eyes instead. "I'm nearly there. However, the tire blew, and I need someone to come and help me change it. Can you recommend someone? I'm not sure the motor association comes out this far."

"Isn't that their job?"

I turned my face away from the oncoming lights. "Good point. And once I hang up, I'd give them a call. I just wanted to let you know I'll be late."

A semi hauling logs drove past me in the opposite direction.

"Just a sec." She covered the phone and her voice muffled, but not enough as her words were easy to understand. "Eric, do you know someone who can change a tire? Oh, of course, why didn't I think of that?" She cleared her throat. "If you drop me a pin, Eric and Mitch can come and change it for you."

"Oh, gosh, that's not necessary."

"You'd rather pay?"

"That's not it." Money wasn't the object; I just didn't want to tear her fiancé and his friend away from their festivities.

"Drop me the pin."

A blinding set of headlights slowed on approach and pulled over to the shoulder, tucking behind my car.

"Just a sec, Lil." I locked my doors for good measure, having read too many horror stories on the internet. "Someone's here."

A heartbeat later, after a door slam, and a silhouette cut through the lights as the figure moved around the back end. It disappeared and a hand tapped on my driver window.

I lowered it just enough and held my phone in front of me. "Lily, hang on. There's a guy here." I stretched out my neck to speak through the three inches of space between the frame and window. "Can I help you?"

He laughed, a deep baritone sound. "Think I should be the one asking you that. Looks like you got a flat."

"I do."

"Want some assistance in changing it?"

"Thanks, my sister's on the phone. I'm just working that out right now."

"Who is it?" Lily asked.

"No idea," I whispered back.

As if I knew. It had been too many years since I'd been out this way, and those I knew had likely left and moved into the big city.

He tugged on his red ball cap and glanced down the road. "Well, I'm here, and I have all the tools needed. Can have you back on the road in five minutes."

Five minutes? That sounded too good to be true. How did I say no to that?

"Okay, thank you. Just a second."

His silhouette reflected once again in the rear view mirror as he walked back to his truck.

"Lil, some guy is going to change my tire. I'll send you my location. If you haven't heard back from me in ten minutes, track me and call the police. However, if this guy's on the up and up, it'll save Eric drive time." Sort of. For now, I was putting the guy into a holding pattern.

"Are you sure?" Her voice had all the hesitation I wanted to unload. No way was I making myself an easy target though.

"I'm sure." I fiddled on my phone and dropped the pin. "Give me ten minutes."

"Fine. I'll be waiting. Stay safe." She clicked off.

I put the phone in an inside pocket to keep it warm and to stop the battery from dying. Inhaling the last of the not yet frozen air, I exited the safety of my car and went to the trunk.

Keeping a safe distance from the interior, lest he toss me in my own trunk, I popped it open and stepped aside.

"I appreciate the help…" I tightened my jacket to the frigid air.

"Name's Jesse." For a heartbeat, he locked his eyes on mine.

"Well, yes, thank you, Jesse, for your assistance. I was driving and suddenly, it just blew." I huddled into my jacket. The air was damp which made the cold seep into the depths of my bones.

"Figured as much when I saw fresh pieces of rubber a little ways back." He reached under the mat and pulled out the spare, leaning it against the side of my car. "Just give me a minute to grab a jack and an impact wrench. Hop in my truck to keep warm."

"No, that's okay." I'd rather shiver uncontrollably than give the stranger any opportunity to kidnap me. Paranoid? Sure, but I was also a realist. "I'll watch, if you're okay with it?"

"Suit yourself." He disappeared into his truck and backed up. Was he taking off?

Instead of driving away, he pulled deeper into the ditch and positioned his truck to light up the passenger side. I wanted to smack myself in the head for being so crazy and had to remind myself not every guy was an asshole. Just most.

A moment later, drill in hand, he stomped through the compact snow to the flat tire.

"Do you want a play by play?" A cheeky hint of a grin tugged on his lips and dimpled the divot in his chin as he positioned the jack under the front end of my car.

"Sure, why not?" I stood on the other side of him so as to not block the bright light while he pumped the jack.

Surprisingly, without an ounce of talking down, he walked me through the easy star pattern of bolt removal and pulled off the shredded mess and the rim, which needed replacing. The dummy tire, as he called it, was pushed into place and the bolts re-fastened.

"All good, miss."

The jack hissed as it lowered my car, and Jesse slid it out.

"Wow, that's it?" I needed to learn how to do that. It looked within my capabilities.

"That's it." He grabbed the shredded tire and set what was

left of it back in my trunk. "You'll need a new one, obviously. Where you headed?"

I swallowed and stared into his eyes. "Cheshire Bay."

"Perfect. There's a shop there, umm, something like Lenny's Neighbourhood Mechanic." He pulled off his cap and gave his head a scratch. "He'll have a small selection of tires, but likely something that'll fit your car."

"Thanks. I truly appreciate your help. What's the charge, and I'll e-transfer you right now." I pulled out my phone, but first, quickly sent a text to Lily, letting her know I would be back on the road within a couple of minutes.

"Nothing, ma'am."

"I have to give you something."

He covered the tire with the mat and closed the trunk lid. "Honestly, it's all good. Pay it forward or something."

I stood there, dumbfounded. "That doesn't feel right."

"What would've been right? Just leaving you here on the side of the road?" He grabbed his jack and drill, setting them into the box of his truck.

Hmm, he got me there. "Well, thank you." The idea of this being a purely sweet gesture wasn't sitting right. "Are you sure?"

Maybe I had some cash in my wallet. It's too bad I hadn't baked anything; those always went over well.

He kept a respectable distance. "Absolutely. You have a Merry Christmas."

"Thank you. You too." I stood there, shivering.

"Get into your car before you freeze to death."

"Thanks again, Jesse."

I hung there on the side of the road until another semi blew past us, the kick up of wind further reducing my internal temperature. With a quick wave, I hopped into my vehicle and started it up, blasting the heat. After rubbing my hands together to return some warm blood into them, I sent another text to Lily and within a moment, I was on my way.

Slowly, I pulled off the side of the road.

Jesse seemed to be following me, but then again, the desolate highway was the only one between Port Alberni and the turn off to Cheshire Bay. I didn't pay it too much attention until he signaled left, like I did, onto the main road leading into the tiny seaside village.

Chapter Two

I t had been a long time since I'd been in Cheshire Bay at Christmas. A lump formed in the back of my throat as I recalled when exactly that was. Mom wanted her last Christmas to be at the beach house; her dying wish. Fourteen years ago, we packed for a couple of weeks to spend Christmas and New Year's at the family home, passed down for a couple of generations.

Sadly, we didn't make it that long.

Mom's health took a turn, and we were home three days before the new year had even started, one person less. After that, I couldn't handle coming back, and used every excuse under the sun to stay home and far away.

Yet, thanks to a wedding my sister was having on Christmas Day, here I was.

After Dad's untimely passing twenty-one months ago, Lily had returned under the assumption of cleaning the place up to sell, but instead she found love in the neighbour next door, Eric. She'd finally found happiness, and deep down, I was truly happy for her.

I flicked on my right turn signal at the major intersection. There were no lights in the small town, and all directions were marked based on right- or left-hand turns. My turn was the second right off Main Street, which was also the second longest road in Cheshire Bay, and the family beach house lay at the very end of it.

Even though I wasn't a Christmas person, the twinkle lights sparkling in every direction were beautiful, as were the lawns decorated with Santas, snowmen, and one purple dragon, a left over from Halloween by the looks of things. The homes were quite different than the condos back in the city. Which I still hadn't told Lily about, and this trip wasn't the right time either.

I glanced into my rear view mirror; Jesse and his truck were still following. Was he afraid another tire would blow? It was too weird.

Cautiously, I continued driving down the lane, watching as Jesse pulled in front of a house three doors down from my childhood summer home. Grabbing my handbag and phone, I exited the vehicle and stared as he ambled over.

The streetlights overhead cast a shadow over his eyes, thanks to the ball cap, but it was still easy to see he was a handsome guy. Broad shoulders, tall, a day's worth of stubble on his face. A gentle swarm of butterflies took flight, and try as I might, I couldn't get them to simmer down. I hadn't felt flurries like that since I'd met my husband, and that was too many years back.

I cleared my throat. "I think I have a stalker." A bubble of a smile formed on my lips against my better judgement.

"Nah." He adjusted his jean jacket and glanced toward the house. "I am as curious about you being ahead of me as you probably are about me following you." He nodded toward the last house. "You're staying at the Bed and Breakfast? Thought it wasn't open yet?"

Right. Lily had mentioned since she was living next door at Eric's, she was turning our old home into a B&B. But not until after the wedding.

"I know the owner."

"Really?" He stepped closer, tipping his head to take me in.

In a small town like this, everyone knows everyone else. And they know your business too. If the population exceeded a thousand people, I'd be shocked. Doubt crept across his features.

For good measure, I pointed. "That used to be my summer home."

"No shit." Jesse stepped back and whistled. "You're here for the wedding?"

"You know about that?" Not that it should've surprised me. Lily probably had the whole area on alert.

"It's Cheshire Bay. *Everyone* knows about that."

"You going?"

He was cute, probably a little younger than me. He could be fun to dance with, maybe have a couple of drinks with, and forget about my skyscraper sized problems.

"Nah. It's a pretty exclusive event."

My heart squeezed a little, figured it was too good to be true. "That sounds like Eric's involvement."

Eric was the calm to the hurricane that was my little sister. Had this been ten, even fifteen years ago, the whole town would've been invited. I, for one, had been intrigued by her changes on her last few visits to Vancouver.

I opened the back door of my car and grabbed a couple of suitcases, setting them on the gravel road.

"Let me help."

"Oh, I'm good, honestly."

But he already had his hands firmly around the handles. "Lead the way." A small, impish smile impossible to ignore settled on his face.

I walked up the sidewalk and hesitated before climbing the stairs. Flashbacks of helping mom down them and into a warmed vehicle smacked me across the face like a cold bite of winter. Had we known in that moment they'd be the last time she graced the landing...

Blinking away the heartache, I shivered.

"Everything okay?"

I inhaled a sharp breath of cool ocean air, readjusting my personal items. "It's just been a while, and I wanted to make sure I had the right address."

It was all lies, but whatever. Finding courage from the depths of my soul, I climbed the four steps and knocked on the door. No answer, so I knocked again with a little more force.

"Mona!" A high-pitched squeal came from beside me. From the house next door. "Let me grab the keys." She walked back inside, but I heard her yell out. "My sister's here."

Eric, her fiancé, came to the door, along with a couple of others I didn't recognize. "Good seeing you again, Mona." He nodded. "Hey, Jesse."

"Eric." Jesse cleared his throat and gave me his full attention, followed by a once over. "So, you're the Mona I've heard rumours about."

My eyes went large, although there was really nothing bad for anyone to remember. That had all been Lily. I was the straight and narrow one. The mother figure type. Old before my time, at least according to the very few friends I had.

"What have you heard?" A slight panic cracked through.

He chuckled, the sweetest laugh I'd heard. "Nothing. Just that the big sister was coming. Remember, small towns talk, and neighbours talk a lot."

Clearly.

My nearly identical sister, albeit a year and a half younger, crossed the tiny stretch of snow-covered grass between the houses and nearly bowled me over with a hug as blonde hairs flew from her face. "I'm so glad you're here."

I patted her back until she broke away. "Me too."

It had been too long. Even though we had lived only a few miles from each other when she had lived in Vancouver, it wasn't until she moved back here and found herself that things between us started improving. She'd grown and matured a lot, and I didn't feel the need to mother her anymore. After all, she was now one herself.

"Oh, hey, Jesse." She straightened her thick sweater.

"Where's Henry?" I'd been dying to see my little nephew.

"Sleeping." She fumbled with the keys and finally, got the right one into the lock, opening the door.

We stepped into the front entrance, cold enough to be mistaken for a large walk-in refrigerator. Our breaths weren't visible, yet, but it was cool enough to know the furnace hadn't been running. For hours at least.

"Oh no."

Lily stormed away to the utility room while I walked down the hall into the living room we once used to hang out in. Only it was different. So different. Long gone were all the knick-knacks and clutter, instead it was calm and homey. It also looked like Beth, her decorator friend, had her hand in the changes. The place was amazing, and seeing it, freed the guilt I'd had about staying here. It looked like any other beach house down this strip, not like a house full of memories, although it was damn cold right now to even make that a possibility.

"The furnace is broken." Lily returned with a pout.

"Are you sure?"

"Yeah, the pilot light won't stay lit."

I was impressed my little sister knew that. I sure as hell didn't. That was Charlie's job. A blue job he called it – one that only men should know how to do. I was relegated to the pink jobs – cooking, cleaning, baby-making. Although I was a complete failure on the last one.

"It's too cold for you to stay here, Mo."

"Why don't you stay at my house for the night?" Jesse's voice called out from the entrance.

I'd totally forgotten he was there. "Oh, thanks. But I'll be fine." Staying at a stranger's house wasn't high on my list of things to do.

Lily jumped in. "She can sleep on the couch." She shrugged and gave me a weak smile. "It's all I've got. There's no spare bed in Henry's room."

I patted her arm. "The couch is more than fine." I'd slept on worst. Especially recently.

Jess cleared his throat. "Don't be ridiculous, Lily. I have a spare room. She can stay there until the furnace is fixed. Then she's not a sudden imposition on you."

"She's never an imposition." But Lily rocked back and forth on her feet, weighing her choices.

However, Jesse was right, like it or not. With her baby and the wedding, the last thing Lily needed was someone in her personal space, something I understood all too well.

I flipped my gaze between the two of them. "I'd hate to impose on you, Jesse, I can get a motel room."

"Have you seen the motels here? They haven't been updated in sixty years, and I think most still have the same original furnishings." He walked to the door and lifted my bags. "I have the space, and it wouldn't be an imposition at all."

My heartbeat quickened. I didn't know this guy from Adam, but he had already come to my rescue once. However, was he safe enough to stay with for the night?

I sent a quick look to Lily, who leaned in close. "He's a good guy. Recently divorced. He's been in Cheshire Bay for years."

Really? "I don't remember a Jesse though."

"That's because he bought the old William's place a few years back. Renovated it too."

"And the wife?"

She lowered her voice even more. "Couldn't handle small town life."

I nodded. Small towns were a complete 180 from a city life, that's for sure.

"I trust him, as does Eric. We've hung out on the beach many times before."

Searching my body and soul for any alarm bells, I gave in with a gentle sigh.

"Don't worry. I won't say anything to Charlie." My sister

patted my arm.

My head bobbed in a way I hoped she understood the importance of keeping her mouth closed.

Not that Charlie would care.

Not anymore, but still.

Heading toward the door, I gave a quick wave to Lily as she locked up.

"I'll call a repairman in the morning, and we'll have you back by tomorrow night." She gave me another hug, and a small kiss graced my cheek. "I'm really glad you're here."

"Get inside. You don't want to catch a cold before your wedding."

She saluted me with a giggle and hopped over to Eric's place – her place. "Why don't you drop your stuff off and come back over for a Christmas drink or something."

"Sure, I'd like that."

I walked down the short sidewalk and joined Jesse. "So, I guess we're temporary roommates?"

"Guess so." He winked. "You don't snore, do you?"

"Oh god, I hope not." The very thought was embarrassing, and now I was terrified of making the unladylike sound. Good thing I'd brought a book to read, so I could stay up late and not fear any kind of deep sleep.

"I'm just kidding. The walls are fairly soundproof."

We walked past Eric's house and his neighbour before

stopping in front of Jesse's.

I hadn't paid any attention on my drive in, but Jesse's place was covered in Christmas decorations. Although the lights weren't turned on, judging by the number of strings and hanging stars, he could give Clark Griswold a serious run for his money.

Lily's house didn't have a speck of Christmas, which suited me just fine, as I didn't celebrate it anyway. But this? Jesse's was way over the top. And if the outside was this grand, what was the inside like?

On second thought, maybe my sister's couch would be better.

Chapter Three

Jesse's floorplan was identical to my childhood beach home, as were all thirteen houses on this final stretch of road, however his spare room was more lavish than some hotel rooms I'd stayed in. There was a gorgeous four-poster bed against the outside wall, a beautiful antique dresser, and a large wardrobe. The only thing throwing off the relaxing vibe of the space was a playpen, folded and tucked off to the side.

"Everything is empty, so please make yourself at home." Jesse leaned against the doorframe. "Unfortunately, it's a shared bathroom, but give me a few minutes to tidy it up, and it'll be fit for a lady."

Before he left with a wink and a spring in his step, I cleared my throat. "Thank you. For putting me up and all."

"Nah, don't worry about it." He eyed the crib in the corner. "It's for when my sister visits. My niece is only a few months old, and boy-oh-boy, can she howl."

Something I'd love to experience. After seven years of trying to have a baby, it looked more and more like my reality was a childless future. Rather than dump that on Jesse, I focused on the suitcases at his feet. "Is she coming for Christmas?"

"Not this year. My brother-in-law got a great job offer in Texas, so they are already down there house hunting."

"Wow. At least it's warm there."

He shrugged, but his expression remained impassive. "It is what it is." He backed away from the door. "I'll let you settle in."

"Lily wants me to come over for a drink. I'm sure she wouldn't mind if you joined us?" It was rude of me to invite him without asking, but my sister loved entertaining, and I was sure another person wouldn't bother her in the least. Especially not a neighbour they hung out with previously.

"After the day I've had, that would be nice. Let me go clean the bathroom first."

"Sure, thanks."

My gaze lingered on him a little longer than it should've as he walked away, but it was impossible to tear my eyes away. Once he removed his ball cap and jean jacket, there was no denying the strong body stretching out the white cotton tee, and a firm ass moving perfectly under his jeans. A full head of sandy blond hair sat squished down and in dire need of a solid fluffing, but yet, it gave him an unexpected charm. He was completely different than my husband.

My soon to be ex-husband.

With a nip in the air, Jesse wore his jean jacket, and I huddled into my thick wool coat. I'd forgotten just how much cooler Cheshire Bay was in winter, and how different the ocean air was here than back home in Vancouver. Here it had a fresh crisp scent, the kind to relax your soul and not have you hold your breath.

We dashed past the darkened windows of the Martin residence, the elderly couple who rented out the home to a variety of guests – all family from their children through the generations to their great-grandchildren. Jesse laughed and stated how hard it was to keep them all straight, because there was always someone there. Except over the holidays, apparently.

We walked up the short sidewalk to Eric's and knocked on the door. Prior to catching up with him when they'd visit me in Vancouver, it had been years since I'd talked with Eric and his brother, Landon, and both had grown from my memory's recollection of awkward and gangly, into strong and handsome men. At least Eric had. I hadn't yet run into Landon, although I expected to see him before the wedding.

I stood on the landing and knocked again, while Jesse hung back a step below.

Lily opened the door with a giant smile on her face. "Come on in, guys."

I wasn't two steps in when she embraced me. It still caught

me off guard as there'd been so many years when she had avoided me, but regardless, I hugged my little sister back until she broke away.

"Come in, come in."

The short strip of hallway led into a decent sized open floorplan of a living room and kitchen. It was also the mirror image to our beach house – well, Lily's now – and it flipped me around. Still, it was homey and inviting in muted shades of greens and taupes, high bar stools, and couches soft and comfortable for sleeping on.

Eric came down the stairs, coming up behind us. "Hey, guys. What can I get you to drink?"

"Something Christmasy," Jesse answered before I had a chance to think.

Eric rubbed his chin and walked into the kitchen while Lily led me over to the couch.

"I'm thrilled you came. Bummer you had to come alone."

I swallowed. "Yeah. Charlie went to Debbie and Doug's." His parents.

They were probably celebrating quite merrily, especially since I wasn't there. Debbie always hated me, and I could never figure out why, but I assumed it was because I couldn't give her only son a child.

"Over Christmas?"

"That was the plan."

My sister's face fell.

"But I wasn't going to miss your wedding, right? He's with his family. I'm with mine." It had been a tough choice too. I had limited options – stay home alone, or drive across the island to a place I really didn't want to see again.

"You're married?" Jesse asked from the kitchen, holding up a glass with a creamy liquid inside as Eric added an amber mixture to it.

I didn't want to spill the beans about my failed marriage, not two days before Lily's big day, so I did what any respectable person would do. I lied. "Yep."

And guzzled down the sweet drink Eric handed to me.

"What happened to your ring?" Lily stared at my naked hand.

Long gone was the natural indent that had occurred from years of wear; my finger filled out as it relished the idea of being free. It took longer for my heart and mind to reach the same agreement.

"It's getting resized." As it sat in the back of my jewelry box.

A smile stretched across her face and she rubbed my arm. "I thought you looked thinner."

It's amazing what getting rid of emotional and physical baggage could do for a person. "Thanks. I am feeling much healthier these days."

She nudged my shoulder and shot a knowing look at my tummy. "Great. Henry needs a little cousin to play with."

My heartstrings vibrated with an ache, and I squeezed my empty glass between my hands trying to diffuse the pain. For a heartbeat, I chanced a glance over to Jesse, who was in deep conversation with Eric over tire repair.

"They're the best on this side of the island." Eric walked over and held his hand above my glass. "Can I get you another, Mona?"

"Sure? Why not? I'm not driving." I needed to drown my sorrows but thankfully I was an upbeat drunk most of the time. A little more alcohol in me and my cares would blow away like dandelion seeds on the breeze.

Eric mixed another drink as Jesse sat in a chair beside me. "So, tomorrow, take your car to Lenny's. I'll leave you the address. He'll get you a proper tire so you're not driving back home on the dummy, and he'll do it at a good price too."

Eric sat beside his wife-to-be. "It may take him a day or two to order it in being the holidays and all."

Lily laughed. "If it's one thing I've learned since moving here, it's how everything runs on *island time*. This ain't no major city."

"Will it be ready by time I need to get back home?"

The plan was to only be here a couple days beyond the big day, and even that was more than I was comfortable with.

"Maybe." Lily giggled.

"Maybe?" I looked between Jesse, Eric, and my sister.

"Let's just say, it'll be a race to see what gets fixed first – your tire or the furnace." She shrugged without a care in the world. At least some things hadn't changed.

I settled back into my chair. "How do you people live this way?"

There was enough of a smile in my words for them to know I was partially kidding. Back home, I'd have a new tire in an hour and a furnace repairperson would already be working on solving the issues there. It's no wonder I never embraced such a laid-back lifestyle. I'd for sure go crazy!

But I was only a guest this visit, and I pitched forward a bit to change the topic. "So, tell me about your wedding plans. What can I do?"

Chapter Four

*A*n hour later, with a couple more drinks poured into me, amazingly enough, I had all the wedding details memorized. It was going to be a simple beach ceremony in front of their place at sunset. Bonfires would spring up along their section of beach with food stations on Eric's and Lily's back patios, and music blasting from the speakers. It sounded more like a beach party from our teens years than it did a wedding ceremony on Christmas Day. However, it sounded perfect for them, and I couldn't wait to be a part of it.

Henry's sudden scream rattled down the stairs, and Lily popped out of her seat. "Sorry. I may be a while. He's been getting these night terrors and it's hard to settle him back down."

"You know what, it's late, Lil. You go take care of your baby, and I'll see you tomorrow."

She gave me a look that was a dead ringer for how my mother used to look at me when I'd volunteer to go and locate Lily at some party. Instant relief. "Thanks, Mo. Night, Jesse."

With a quick wave, she disappeared down the short hall and up the stairs to her wailing son.

As I pushed myself up, my body felt as if it weighed 300 pounds and it took me more time than I'd like to get to a standing position. Perhaps I should've moved more rather than sit as still as a statue and pour back those merry drinks. I shook my head, which was the wrong thing to do as the room started spinning, and I tossed my arms out the side.

"Whoa." Jesse jumped beside me. "A little too much to drink?"

I stared at his handsome face. He had a lot of scruff, that sexy 5 o'clock kind, and I wanted to run my hand over it. However, according to everyone in the room, I was still a married woman, and it would've been highly inappropriate.

"Nope." I popped the *p*. "I had just the right amount, thank you, and I'm feeling pretty good." I tried to whisper.

Eric laughed. "Well, those were some highly tainted drinks."

I thrust a thumbs up sign and smiled. At least I thought it was a smile. "Awesome. Just what I needed."

Jesse had an arm wrapped around my waist. "Let's get you back to my place."

His gaze pulled me close, and along with drowning my sorrows, the alcohol smothered my inhibitions. "Okay," I breathed out as a sly grin stretched across my lips. It was far too easy to stare into those dark brown eyes, the irises lined with a halo of amber.

"Need a hand?" Eric asked.

"Why? I can walk on my own two feet." I stood straight just to prove my point and then tittered to the left and caught myself against Jesse's firm chest.

Jesse gripped my waist tighter as he answered Eric. "I'm good, man. It's a short walk."

A short walk that somehow seemed to take the better part of ten minutes because I couldn't get enough of the twinkling lights in his yard and needed to stand and watch, mesmerized.

"They're so pretty."

"I'm glad you think so. C'mon. It's getting cold out."

Reluctantly, I let him lead me inside where indeed it was nice and warm. There was a hint of redness on his cheeks, and a sparkle in his eyes that matched the lights outside.

"It's been quite the day, hasn't it?" Jesse shrugged out of his jacket and helped me out of mine.

"Yeah. I locked all my belongings into my new place before I headed here. I hadn't even unpacked. Movers left the boxes, and without a thought of what to do with my life now, here I came."

"A new place is always nice." Jesse pointed towards the stairwell. "Up we go."

"Did you know I've never lived on my own?" I stepped on the first stair and contemplated the second. "Left home for college with roommates, and left college for Charlie, and now, I'm in my own place."

I leaned against the wall after climbing four stairs. It required too much energy, and the little I had left I wanted to save for the climb into bed. Waiting a minute wasn't going to hurt anything. Besides, I needed to catch my breath. I started sliding down the wall to rest on the stair.

"Oh no. Only a few more to go." Jesse reached for my hand and gave it a gentle tug. "C'mon. You're almost there."

The alcohol seemed to give a voice to the words I'd held back for so long, and a little misdirection from the sweet guy wasn't going to stop me.

"It was over between us for so long. He'd already moved out but graciously offered to let me stay in the house until it sold. Wasn't that nice of him?" The last three stairs were the hardest, but I gave it my best with Jesse's tugs and stood at the top victorious. "Ta-da." My arms flew out to the sides. "Isn't Charlie the best?"

"I honestly wouldn't know." He walked me to the door of my temporary lodgings. "Are you okay to … you know… take care of getting ready for bed?"

"Oh yeah. I'll be fine. Thanks for your help." I stepped into the room. "G'nite, Jesse."

I slumped onto the bed and the room darkened.

# # #

I woke with a throbbing headache. What the hell had I done last night? And what was worse, what had I unloaded on Jesse? Faint memories tickled my thoughts and slowly, the realization of it came to fruition. I had confessed about my failed marriage. To a stranger. I hadn't even told my own sister.

I sat up in bed, and after seeing it was after eight, listened. Aside from the faint rolling sound of waves crashing on the shore, there didn't seem to be any other sound in the house. No movement, no shuffling of feet, not even a snore. After freshening up in a very neat and tidy bathroom, I inched my way downstairs and into the hall.

"Good morning." Jesse's low voice called out from the living room.

"Morning." I averted his gaze and kept my head down low.

He rose off his seat, after folding the newspaper in half.

"There's fresh coffee brewed and a bottle of Tylenol beside it. Help yourself to anything. Sorry that there's not a lot of fresh food." He opened a tiny drawer beside the fridge and pulled out a scratch pad and pen, along with a keychain. In terrible chicken scratch, he wrote down a name and address. "This is Lenny's place. If you're not familiar, it's just off the main drag, tucked closer to the wharf."

I was sure the locations in the Bay would come back to me once I drove around.

"And here's a key so you can come and go."

I stared at it as it skittered across the island. "But you don't... I'm a..."

35

CHRISTMAS in CHESHIRE BAY

"You're Lily and Eric's sister. That's enough for me. Besides, small towns talk, right?" His empty coffee cup rattled in the sink as he set it down.

I nodded. Slowly. "About last night…"

"I promise to not say a word." He gave me another once over but settled his gaze on my face. "I need to work for a bit today, but I should be back by two."

"What do you do?"

He hesitated, and his mouth opened quickly and shut with a snap.

"Sorry, I was being nosey. You don't need to answer." I wrapped my fingers around the keychain and lifted it into the air, still avoiding eye contact. "I promise to guard it with my life."

He moved a couple feet closer toward the front door and stopped. "Would I be out of line to see if you wanted to go to dinner tonight?"

I blinked twice and looked into his eyes, feeling a gentle pull into them. "No. Not at all."

"Perfect. I'll see you later."

With that, he left his house, leaving me alone. As my stomach growled, I inched open the fridge to see what was quick to grab for a bite to eat. He wasn't kidding when he said there wasn't much; it was nearly empty. I did a little poking around his bare cupboards, noting a few things while setting up a small list of items to buy.

Assuming there was still a grocery store in town, I was going

36

to stock his fridge and pantry full. After all, he'd put me up for a night, and had helped me with a flat tire. It was the very least I could do, and I hoped I wasn't overstepping.

Once, when I was down on my luck my first semester in college, my dad had done it for me. Dead broke, my roommates and I couldn't even scrap together enough cash between the three of us to buy a bag of apples and a jug of milk. Dad took it upon himself to fill our cupboards and fridge and freezer. To this day, I've never forgotten how savoury a fresh apple was and how wonderful it felt to not have to eat another bag of cheap ramen, which incidentally I noted Jesse had a small stash of.

After meeting with Lenny, I wasn't too comfortable with going back to Jesse's house and just hanging out, so I walked the main drag in Cheshire Bay wondering how much things had changed. Spoiler alert, nothing had. The store names remained the same, all funky little town Mom & Pop types of names; Belles et Garcons, Daisy's Delights, Sylvia's Bakery. All stores I remember visiting when I was in my teens, especially the bake shop with its gigantic cinnamon buns.

As the snow fell in picturesque flakes, Christmas carols played from some mystical places, as I never saw any speakers. The storefronts all had a holiday display of some sort, whether it be holly and berries, or angels, or a nicely painted Christmas tree.

It was overload though, and the thought of hearing '*Have Yourselves a Merry Little Christmas*' was enough to make me leave.

I couldn't be the only one in town who didn't enjoy Christmas, and yet, as I scanned the street, people were chatting with smiles and friendly pats as their arms were loaded up with bags.

Maybe I *was* the only one.

I popped into *Whimsical Whims*, a tchotchke paradise. The window display promised something for everyone, and I appreciated a good challenge. Near the front of the store there were a variety of handmade ornaments, and I searched the tree for a better part of a half hour looking for the perfect gift for Lily, testing the stores promise. In addition to the sizeable cheque for her wedding gift, I wanted to find a nice ornament to bestow upon her as a memento of the season. Mom had always given us a special one for the tree every year since I was born, until... she couldn't.

While I was on the hunt for Lily in a half-hearted effort to reboot the tradition, I stumbled across one for Jesse - a twinkling Christmas tree that reminded me of his front yard. I held the lightweight ornament in my palm and in doing so, spied the gift beckoning me. Buried into the branches was a silver snowflake baring an etched sentimental saying about the love and bond between sisters. It was too perfect to not get it, even if Lily and I weren't quite there in our relationship, it was certainly on its way.

I took both up to the register, stopping at another display case filled with hand-carved wooden ornaments. "These are gorgeous."

Despite the multitude of options, I selected a 2D snow globe and added it to the two others.

"Would you like this engraved?" The teenaged boy asked as he pulled out a pile of tissue paper. "It would go here." His nail-bitten fingertip touched the bottom.

"Sure." I tipped my head to the side in deep thought and glanced to the display, hoping there was a sign or something to give me a spur of the moment idea. There was nothing. "What about 'The Morris Family' and add the year?"

It should work. Something to commemorate their Christmas Day wedding.

"Sure thing, ma'am. It'll take about an hour for Gus to do it."

"That's fine."

I was getting some tummy growlies and wanted to grab a bite to eat anyway. I paid for the gifts, and tucked my receipt into my purse, and held the little bags in my hand.

Exiting Whimsical Whims and away from Mariah Carey's only holiday hit, I spotted Jesse walking across the street.

"Hey!" I waved.

He crossed over the street after a sedan passed, a smile leaking slowly off the edges of his pinkish pout. "Doing some shopping?"

"Well, you know. Keeping the locals in business." I lifted the couple of bags. It wasn't much really. I'd spent most of my money so far buying groceries.

"That's kind of you, and I'm sure they all appreciate it. Where you heading next?"

I looked up and down the street. "Peter's Pitas. Lenny went on and on about them."

The older man had a wrapped order on his desk and even through the wax paper, the hint of spices and cooked meat was mouth-watering. I didn't need his accolades, but it sure helped in securing a place to have lunch.

"They're just up here, off the drag."

"Do you have time to join me?"

He nodded and checked his watch. "I'll need to be back in the office at one for a quick order arrival, but yeah, I have time."

"Sounds fun."

He was dressed pretty casually in jeans and a sweater, so not likely an office job. Maybe he worked at one of the little indie businesses? Or helped fill shelves at the grocer, although I would've seen him this morning.

Jesse stood a little straighter. "Not really. I have a shipment of urns coming in."

My face fell.

"I'm a mortician."

Chapter Five

Jesse being a mortician was not the job I expected him to have. Not at all.

"It's okay, I get that a lot." An impassive expression settled over his face.

"What's that?"

He circled my head with a long finger. "That blank stare."

I shook away the look and tossed my gaze to the sidewalk which was decorated with a fresh covering of snow smooshed into the sidewalk. "Sorry."

"What's to be sorry for? Sure, it doesn't have the glamour and prestige of a doctor or a lawyer…"

"Or an accountant." I winked, understanding exactly what he meant. "I get it. No one grows up saying they'll be an accountant or a mortician."

"It's a dead-end job, I agree." He chuckled.

I laughed and nearly snorted from his bad joke. "That's

funny."

"Well, if I don't keep it light, then the dreariness will bury me."

"Oh stop." I grabbed his arm to balance myself.

He pulled me out of the way of a passerby. "Afternoon, Mrs. Thornsbird." He tipped his head in the direction of the older lady. "Merry Christmas."

I straightened myself up and inhaled a sharp sigh, collecting my wits. "My apologies."

"Don't please. Humour is important, and besides, you have a great laugh."

"You think so?" Heat blossomed on my cheeks as my smile pushed the apples higher. My laugh had always grated on Charlie's nerves.

"I do." There was more sincerity behind his eyes than I'd seen before. And it was directed at me. A first, for sure. "Care to grab some lunch?"

I nodded and followed his lead. We walked down the main street and turned onto another which was still part of what could be considered downtown Cheshire Bay. Peter's Pitas was on the right and a jingling of bells overhead announced our arrival.

A silver haired man with a beard that would give Santa Claus a run for his money walked up to the counter.

"Season's Greetings. What can I getcha?" He washed his hands at the small sink.

"I'll have a number three," I said after studying the menu.

So many mouth-watering choices. I was going to have to come back here again before I went home.

"What about you?" I nudged Jesse.

"The number six please. No tomatoes though. I'm allergic."

"No problem." He got to work assembling our lunches.

Internally I smacked my forehead. Allergies. Hadn't even given that a speck of thought while grocery shopping.

"Do you have any other food restrictions?"

He leaned against the counter. "Just tomatoes."

A loud sigh rolled out as I shifted my bags into my other hand. "Thank goodness."

"Why?" His brows pinched together.

"I kind of did something this morning."

"What? What did you do?" His eyes danced as his gaze jumped around.

Not sure how he would take it, I stepped back a little, putting a smidgen of distance between us. Not that I expected him to take a swing at me or anything. "I bought some groceries for your fridge and pantry. As a thank you for putting me up last night and listening to me go on and on about things."

"You didn't need to do that." But there was a gratefulness in his tone. One I remembered from my roommates when they said thanks to my dad.

The decoy Santa wiped his hands on his apron and set our

food on a tray. "Sixteen-fifty, please."

Jesse reached for his wallet, but I beat him to it and handed my card to the silver-haired man.

"I insist."

I smiled and slid my card into the machine before I heard another peep. "I insist more."

"Thanks again," Jesse said as he slowly pushed the wallet back into his jeans. "But it should really be me."

"No, it shouldn't. I lived with a very Archie Bunker-like man for ten years, and I don't mind picking up the tab for this." I grabbed the tray full of food and walked over to an empty table.

Jesse sat across from me and slowly unwrapped his pita. "Although it's not my place to ask, but I'm dying to know. Based on last night's stairwell conversation, why doesn't Lily know?"

I sighed. "Lily and I are complicated."

"Aren't all families?" He snickered.

I shrugged and unwrapped my pita, folding over the edges of the wax paper slowly and methodically. "Have you always lived in Cheshire Bay?"

"Nah. Moved here a few years back." He took a hearty bite of his food.

"Well then, you didn't know Lily when she was a teen?" I stared at the napkin as he dragged it across his mouth – lucky napkin.

Jesse stared deep into my eyes.

"She was always a wild child. Rebellious wouldn't even be

the right word. Lily and Mom disagreed on just about everything right from the get-go, and Dad didn't want to ruffle the already ruffled feathers, so he stayed out of things. But oh boy, she was a bad kid. Always drinking and doing drugs, defying curfew, that kind of thing." I shook my head from the memories, unable to stop sharing once I got going. "It was way worse when we were here for the summer as she was the most popular kid in the Bay area from the time she was eleven or so. By then, my parents had pretty much given up on her for those months and allowed her free reign, so to speak." Until I needed to go and rescue her.

Jesse's jaw hit the table. "You'd never know it now."

There was something comforting about Jesse, something allowing me to talk about the past without fear of being ridiculed or highly judged.

I hadn't had a connection like that with another adult in years, and it egged me on to spill more. "No. She's turned her life around, and I'm very proud of her." I fiddled with my drink and finally pulled back the tab. "But when Mom first got sick, Lily was only fourteen. And if rules were made to be broken beforehand, there was no way her sickness was going to make anything better. So... I stepped up since Dad was too busy taking care of Mom."

"Sounds like you had to."

"Maybe. Maybe not. Maybe she would've been fine. I'll never know." It wasn't ideal in the least. "But I spent most of my summers trying my damnedest to keep trouble away from Lily, but it still found her. She did drugs, and smoked a lot, and had more sex before the age of sixteen than I've had in my married life. And she spent most of her teenage years hating me."

Jesse cast his gaze to the basket of fries and pulled one out, popping it into his mouth.

Yeah, I'd look away too. And I did. I took a quick sip of my drink and stared at the counter where the Decoy Santa was crafting another order.

"Anyways, our relationship was very one-sided. I was always watching out for her, mothering her, if you will. Even when I stopped coming to the beach house after Mom died, I was still her mother-figure. We both knew that. I wasn't her sister. I didn't confide anything to her, and whatever she shared with me, I already knew thanks to social media. I was the last person she confided in. When my marriage fell apart, I couldn't admit to anyone. You're the…"

No one at work knew, and no one questioned anything when I needed to change my direct deposits. I didn't even have the heart to tell Jesse he was the first to know. How sad was that?

"Sounds like you grew up before your time."

"Maybe." I took a small bite and chewed carefully.

"It's not my place to ask, but since you're sharing… While you were busy caring for your sister, and your dad was busy caring for your mom, who was busy taking care of you?"

I pushed back against the plastic backrest and stared – not a harsh stare, but one of complete astonishment. My heart squeezed a little bit as memories flipped through my mind.

"I was old enough to take care of myself." Which was true. I pretty much had been since my middle teens.

"You're what, two years older than Lily?"

"Eighteen months."

He chewed a few more fries, heavily coating them in ketchup, and then took another bite of his pita.

"I know what you're thinking."

Finally, his gaze connected with me. "I highly doubt it but try me."

However much I wanted to, I couldn't give voice to the words. They were all there in my mind, but were swirling around so much, they'd never find an exit, at least not one that made any sense.

Instead of speaking, I sighed and stacked my fries, sprinkling them with a fresh dusting of seasoning salt. "Regardless of what happened back then, I simply can't tell Lily my marriage ended months ago. Not yet. She has a sweet son and a doting husband and is getting married in two days."

"You don't think she'd care to know about your… situation? Maybe the tables have turned, and it's her turn to take care of you."

I shook my head. "Although she's grown up, and she's not as wild as she was, I don't want to burden her with that kind of news."

"How long do you think it'll be before she puts the pieces together herself? This Charlie can't be on vacation or business trips forever, right?"

47

He was right, of course. The last two times we've gotten together, Charlie was absent, and while Lily may have been a wild child, she was pretty smart.

"Someday I'll tell her, just not right away. She deserves a wedding day free of drama."

"Said like a doting big sister." He winked and continued to devour his food. "How long were you and Charlie married?"

"Ten years." I took another bite and swallowed, wanting to ask him the same thing. "Lily mentioned you're recently divorced?"

"See? Small towns talk." He nodded, making me feel like a huge idiot. A huge *gossiping* idiot. However, he ignored it and carried on. "Member of the Divorce Club. After four years of unwedded bliss."

I wanted to laugh at the tone of his voice, but it wasn't right. Instead, I covered his hand with mine. "I'm sorry. It sucks, right?"

"I'm used to shrugging it off because most don't get it and have the best of intentions when they say it takes two to ruin a marriage, right?" He looked deep into my eyes. "But, yeah, it sucked."

"Did she cheat?"

His gaze raked me over, as if studying to guess how I'd react. "That would probably make it easier, but no, she fell out of living the small-town life. She hated it, but we moved here because that's where the job was, and as sole supporter, it's my job to provide for her and take care of her. Besides, I figured the change would be good for us. Get away from her meddling family who were constantly asking from the moment we said 'I do' if we were pregnant yet." He shook his head and let his focus fall to the salt and pepper shakers.

There was a lot of vitriol in his words, but I let him spew it out, pretty sure he wasn't going to hold back either.

"All her parents wanted was a grandchild even though they'd never really accepted me into the family, and they were embarrassed to tell people what I did for a living. I think, at one point, they said I was in real estate." He laughed a sad, painful laugh and pushed the tray off to the side. "Her previous boyfriends were all executives and doctors. I never knew what she found in me, but whatever it was, it wasn't enough to keep her around. She got what she wanted and left."

"I'm so sorry. Life's unfair, isn't it?" My heart ached hearing his story, and I searched his face for the answer clearly settling across it.

"Want to go for a walk? I feel I've brought this lunch down into misery."

"Misery is my middle name, didn't you know? Mona Misery Baker." I almost tacked on my married name, but since I was at the start of all the paperwork to remove it, now was a good time to stop announcing it.

The weak joke worked. A small grin played over his lips, but it didn't turn into anything bigger. Instead, he rose and tossed our garbage away.

"Merry Christmas, Pete." He waved at the silver-haired man.

"Merry Christmas, Jesse."

The bells jingled overhead, and we stepped outside, back into the fresh ocean air.

Across the road, carollers sang. Real people dressed in long robes with top hats and bonnets, holding leather-bound songbooks in their hands. I blinked several times to make sure it was real.

"Let's go listen. It'll be good to hear the merriment and joy."

No way was I going to get much closer. Carolers were not my thing, just like the whole of the holiday season. However, before I could put the brakes on, Jesse was tugging me across Main Street.

Chapter Six

I didn't sing along with the carolers, but Jesse sure did. He was tone deaf and off key, but clearly didn't care. It was charming, if not a little hard to listen to, but I found myself entranced watching him feel the words and sing with all his heart.

He stepped back to me when the carolers closed their books and moved further down the street. "Sorry, I just love that song. Couldn't help myself."

Never again will I be able to hear 'Deck the Halls' without seeing Jesse giving it his all.

"How come you weren't singing?"

"Too busy taking in the moment."

His gaze roamed up and down, and he tipped his head to the side. "Hmm… Okay." He checked his watch. "Oh, shoot. I need to go. See you back at my place in a bit?"

I understood the need to go, but if I was being honest, I didn't want him to leave.

"Sure thing. I need to pick up a couple of items and then go pick up my car." I shifted my bags into my other hand.

He paused and stepped closer. "What did Lenny say?"

"He'll have a tire for me on the twenty-seventh."

"Wow, although that's expected. This isn't a major city."

"Yeah. He said he's going to the mainland for the holiday, but he'll be back on the twenty-sixth and will install a fresh set the next morning. After that, I'll be good to go."

It was only four days from now, and with Christmas and a wedding, no doubt the time would fly by anyway.

"Perfect." Jesse stood there, rocking back and forth.

"I'm keeping you. Go."

He rocked forward once again; mouth slightly parted as if he had something to say. Instead, he took off with a wave. "See you around two."

He crossed the street and hustled down it, turning the corner.

So far, having lunch with Jesse counted as the best lunch date I'd had in months. Years even.

I pulled in front of Jesse's house shortly after two and was just replying to a couple of emails when his red pickup came into sight.

He hopped out and did a double take at me sitting in my car, so I closed out of my phone and got out. "You know you're welcome to go in. That's why I gave you a spare."

"And I did." Earlier. "But I just got here and had to answer a few things."

We walked to the steps and he unlocked the door, opening it for me to go into first. I hung back near the entrance, methodically hanging my jacket in the closet as he headed into the kitchen, unsure of what his true reaction would be to the groceries.

"Damn," he drawled out and whistled as he took in the full pantry, fridge, and a giant bowl of fresh fruit. "This must've set you back a fortune."

"It wasn't that bad." For a small-town grocery store. It was nuts though for city prices. "Besides, you're going to get scurvy if you don't get enough vitamin C, so there are plenty of oranges and apples and grapefruit to get you through the next few days."

"I do love a good mandarin." He grabbed a green tissue paper wrapped orange from the bowl on his island. "Care for one?"

"Sure." I snatched it from the air with a perfect catch. Peeling it, the citrus smell bloomed in the air and put a spring in my step.

"You really didn't have to do this, you know."

I swallowed down a hearty bite. "I swear I didn't mind. My dad did it once for me, and I know what it's like to be down a little."

"I'll be paid at the end of the month. I had enough food." His tone turned defensive as he leaned against the cupboards.

"Sorry, I didn't mean to overstep." I backed away, wondering where I should go. Up to my room? Back out to the car? Maybe over to Lily's?

"Hey, I'm the one who's sorry." He crossed his arms over his tight chest and a sadness creased the corners of his eyes. "I'm just not used to having someone do things like this. Not for me."

A smile leaked out the edges of my lips. "Ditto."

He inched his way toward me. "Business isn't too busy these days, which really is a good thing. Means people are healthier and taking care of themselves."

"That is a good thing." Until I remembered his job. If no one was dying, then he wasn't busy, and if he wasn't busy, then the income was likely a reflection of that. "Ah," I said in understanding.

"In the meantime, I've been working at the tree farm on the edge of town, but that's starting to wrap up with the end of the season. Not too many people buying Christmas trees two days before the big day. But I swear I can pay you back."

"Jesse," I said, putting my proverbial foot down but my hand on his strong arm. "It was a gift, so no, you may not pay me back."

Sincerity flowed out in my words and bounced back in the form of a warm smile stretching across Jesse's face.

"Well..." He inhaled. "Thank you very much. I truly appreciate it."

It was clear to see he did. "My pleasure." My shoulders fell and my soul had an extra beat to it. I was happy to help him out. It felt good to return the favour. "So, since we have some time to kill before I whip you a fabulous supper, what are some fun things to do around here? I'm sure things have changed quite a bit since my teenage years."

"Do you know how to skate?"

We parked his red pickup in the parking lot of the only school in town and exited. A small shack had been erected at the edge of the lot, along with dozens of benches. I rented some skates and pulled my toque down low enough to cover my ears, hopefully giving me a wee bit of cuteness before we pushed off from the bench.

It had been years since I'd donned a pair of skates, but like the proverbial saying – it was just like riding a bike. After a couple of glides and some wiggly arms to help me regain my balance, I found my groove.

Jesse, on the other hand, looked as if he was born on skates. Every push off seemed effortless, and he flipped from skating forward to gliding in reverse with ease.

"You're good at this." As my own glides lacked the strength to get me very far. I had to skate twice as hard as him to keep up.

"I come here all the time. It's great exercise and it's a good way to burn off the doldrums of the day."

"I can only imagine. Seeing people in deep sadness and overwhelming grief must be draining." I ran out of energy and plopped myself down on a bench.

Jesse sprayed ice to the edge of the rink as he came to a halt and joined me. "It can be. But I try not to take it personally. If I can work in the background and make sure everything is as perfect as can be, I call it a win. I don't need to interact with the mourners, and only need to meet with the loved ones when we are making the arrangements."

"With your compassion, I'm sure they appreciate all that you do."

A faint blush reddened his cheeks, and he tugged on his mittens. "I just try to treat people how they deserve to be treated. With dignity and respect."

A teenage boy skated by. "Hey, Mr. Lancaster."

"Merry Christmas, Jordan." He turned back to me. "He works at the grocer. Small town, right?"

"Very much so. I live in Vancouver, and I wouldn't be able to guess the names of those who bag my groceries or pour my coffee."

"Quite different though. Turnover is probably pretty high, but here, people tend to keep their jobs as job possibilities aren't endless." He waved at another skater.

"Where did you live before you moved here?"

"Richmond."

"That's pretty big. Lots of jobs there."

He shrugged. "Maybe now. But not a few years ago. And definitely not in my field. What about you? Did you give up being a full-time homemaker and are now just starting out in accounting?"

Having rested, I patted his thigh and pushed myself back onto the two blades.

"C'mon. I'll race you." I scrambled to dig my toe pick in and go as fast as I could around the oval, but it wasn't a few strides until I heard the telltale sound of blades scraping across the ice as Jesse caught up.

"I didn't mean to offend you by asking."

"You didn't." I forced a smile and found a nice easy rhythm to skate to as I buried down the nagging heartache. "I'm just not a homemaker." And will never be. That implied children. Something I could never produce. "I'm actually a controller."

Jesse's sweet laugh was music to my ears. "I don't know what that is, but it sounds like something I can see you doing. You do like to be in control."

Laughing and skating at the same time were too much for me to handle, and I waved my arms rapidly to prevent a fall. Luckily though, Jesse was right there to steady me.

"Thanks." I cast my gaze downward for a heartbeat before I explained. "I oversee the financial reports and help the company budget their money."

It had been a hard fought for dream because after we got married, Charlie insisted I stop working full time. Thankfully, I had managed part time for a few years, and a year ago, after the devastating news I would never carry a child, I went full time. The title made it sound like a bigger deal than it really was.

"So, you're really good with money?"

"I guess."

We moved around the ice, and every once in a while, I flung my arms out for balance.

"You can hold my hand, if it helps?" He extended his mittened hand.

I stared with disbelief and excitement. It was a weird feeling, but I grasped his hand with a strong grip. A lap around while holding hands was nice. Too nice, and when I stopped to rest against a stack of hay bales, Jesse stood in front of me. His cheeks were red from the cool air, and his eyes had a warmth to them. There was a certain charm in his grin as his gaze danced over my face.

"You're really something, you know?"

But I didn't. All my married life, it wasn't something I knew. Charlie wasn't forthcoming with compliments, and only in recent months had I tried to figure out what it was about him I'd been so drawn to originally. Over time, the looks had faded, mainly because his true personality took over. He wasn't mean or anything, but he wasn't a classifiable sweetheart either. He used to be a fun seven, but over time fell to a meh five or six on his better days.

And Jesse? In the short time I'd know him, he was already a strong eight, maybe even a nine. He was…

I blinked and studied the man staring at me, wondering what those lips would taste like, and curious about how he kissed. Would they be strong or soft yet firm? Was he the type of kisser who could weaken my knees and light me on fire? I wanted to feel myself pressed into him, his arms wrapped around me, and have the world fade away. But I couldn't. Wouldn't.

It wasn't … right? No, that's wrong, because I hadn't felt as comfortable with anyone as I have been with Jesse. Maybe it was the lack of knowledge to the outside world of my failings. Maybe it was shame that I couldn't keep Charlie and I together, and no longer wanted to. The nagging doubt reminding me if I couldn't make that work, how could I ever make something new work?

But those eyes of Jesse's. They stared right into the depths of my soul. His head was tipped to the side and a shy grin tickled the left side of his lips, making it twitch. And I wanted to, wanted to give in to the racing pulse and the adrenaline coursing through me. I rolled in the side of my bottom lip, and heartbroken at my lack of courage, pushed away.

Even though I couldn't, a smile crossed my face and my confidence blossomed from the way Jesse had raked me in. It had been too long since I'd felt like that, so bravely, I attempted to spin like Jesse had and tried skating backwards. Instead, my skates slipped out from under me, and my butt cracked against the surface of the ice. I tossed my head back in pain.

Jesse put his skate in front of mine and offered a strong hand, pulling me up effortlessly, the light in his gaze shining as brightly as a star. His charm oozed and once again, an overpowering urge to kiss him consumed me.

59

"Should we take these off now?"

Stabbing pain shot down my left leg reminding me I wasn't in a Hallmark movie.

"Probably. I need to be able to walk my sister down the beach and give her away." Like a child's first time on skates, I shuffled towards the nearest bench. So much for romance and fun.

"You're giving Lily away? That's really cool."

"I'm the only family she has left. Would be weird of Eric's step-dad to do it."

"I suppose." Jesse helped me onto the bench and bent down to untie my skates.

"Speaking of my sister, I have a plus one going unused. Interested?"

A long, hardened stare back responded to my invite as he bore into my soul. "And you don't think that would help your sister jump to conclusions?"

He was right. If I didn't tell my sister what was up in my life, it would look really suspicious to bring a stunningly handsome guy to a wedding who was not my ex-husband, even if I really wanted him there. To dance in his arms. To take in the surf. To walk in the moonlight. To be wild and carefree for the first time in my adult life.

I hung my head and sighed as the skates slipped off.

My phone buzzed in my pocket, and I checked on the caller ID. "It's Lily." Jesse sat beside me while I answered. "Hey."

"Hey, Mo. Listen, I have bad news."

My eyes went large, and my stomach tightened. "What's wrong?"

"Oh, nothing. Nothing major, really." She was stalling. "Umm… the furnace guy was here to look at the, well, the furnace. He says the motor's shot."

"That happens all the time."

"Yeah, well, this isn't YVR." Speaking in airport code was something I wasn't used to. "He can't get the part in until after Christmas, and maybe not even until the new year."

"Oh?"

"So, we're going to clear the couch and make things as comfy as possible." There was hesitation in her voice, a reluctance as if my being a guest in her living room was more than just an inconvenience.

"Lil, don't worry about it. I can get a motel here."

From the corner of my eyes, Jesse shook his head, so I turned in his direction.

He leaned his forearms on his thighs.

"The motels here are gross. Tell Lily you're staying at my place. As long as you need." There was a finality in his voice, but it wasn't one that scared me.

"I couldn't impose on you like that," I said to Jesse, tipping the phone away from my mouth.

"Trust me, it's not an imposition."

"Are you with Jesse?" A pitch at the end of her sentence had me back peddling. Fast.

"Well not with him with him. We're just out and about." I scrunched my face.

"I certainly wasn't implying you were *with him* because that would be weird being married and all. And besides, it's Jesse." She said it like he was a tattered hand-me-down or something, and her wording and tone rubbed me the wrong way.

I sighed, stuck between a rock and hard place. Jesse wasn't Charlie, not even close, and yet my sister who didn't know any better, was taking the side of the guy I was no longer married to. Perhaps it would be better to come out and tell the truth. My mouth opened to speak, but words failed to emerge.

"Anyway, about your lodgings…"

"Lil, we'll figure out something, but don't worry, okay? I'm going to be the least of your concerns. You have a wedding in less than 48 hours. That deserves your full concentration, not my accommodations."

A sigh breezed over the line. "Thanks. Mo. Tell Jesse he should come for the ceremony and party. It'll be fun and he can take Charlie's seat, since he's not coming."

I tipped my head to the side and smiled at my temporary roommate. "I'll tell Jesse he's been invited. Thanks."

A self-assured grin stretched across my face. Having him there wouldn't be weird at all anymore. But I still needed to tell my sister what was going on in my life at some point.

Lily interrupted my train of thought. "Are you coming for

breakfast tomorrow?"

"Wouldn't miss it." I had placed an order with the bakery for a variety of pastries. After all, the whole wedding crew would be there.

"See you in the morning."

I hung up and pocketed my phone, all the while unable to wipe the stupid grin on my face. "Problem solved. So, as I was asking before... Are you interested in coming to a beach wedding on Christmas Day?"

Chapter Seven

*A*fter a filling dinner of bibimbap, one of my specialities since it's easy to make and it's fairly healthy, Jesse topped up our wine glasses. This time, I went easy on the drinking. I didn't want another unloading of my secrets on the unsuspecting victim.

We moved from the kitchen to the living room, which is to say, we moved about ten feet. The house wasn't huge, but cozy in size. And since most residents on the strip used their homes during the summer, time wasn't spent in the house. Why would you with the ocean steps away?

"Care to watch a movie?" He grabbed the remote off the bookshelf.

"As long as it's not a Christmas movie." The words were out before I could stop them. Maybe I *had* drank too much wine.

"Something against a good holiday classic?" He stood impossibly close, and his gaze flittered between my eyes as if searching for the truth I'd never admit.

My bottom lip rolled between my teeth. "Well, it's just that…" There was no good way of answering. I tossed my hands out to the side. "By this time in the season, I've watched them all."

"Do you have a favourite? We could always watch that one."

None of them were. They were all so happy and lovey-dovey with everything ending up perfect for the main characters. Real life never worked out that way. People died on Christmas Day, forever changing the way the holiday was meant to be. My sister was a prime example. How many people actually got married on Christmas Day rather than sitting around the base of a decorated tree unwrapping presents? Probably none.

Jesse grabbed a couple of blankets from the back of the couch. "What if instead of watching a movie, we just sat outside on the deck. I've got a space heater to take the edge off. And we don't even have to talk."

I breathed a sigh of relief and reached for one of the blankets, my fingers grazing his arm. My synapses went on a wild spree with the delicate touch. "That sounds heavenly."

After he turned off the overhead lights, the only glow in the room was from the lights heavily decorating the tree. The space under the tree was lacking presents. With his family out of town, had he mailed them out? Up until that moment, I had suspected he'd be celebrating Christmas morning with *someone*. But as I gazed again at the empty tree skirt, an ache formed in my heart.

"You coming?" Jesse asked, and I whipped my focus over to

him, where he stood at the door waiting.

Once outside, he pulled an Adirondack style chair over and gave it a quick dusting.

"Sorry. I don't get much company these days."

I curled into the seat and covered myself with the waffle-weave blanket and set my wine glass on the armrest as Jesse turned on the patio heater. Instantly a wave of warmth settled over me, and I let out a low groan. "That's nice."

He sat and took a sip of wine. "It's a nice evening."

Indeed, it was. The surf was crashing just out of sight but well within listening range. That was the best part of Cheshire Bay, in my humble opinion. The houses on this strip had some of the finest beaches on the island, and since it was the Pacific Ocean as far as the eye could see, the waves were free to make as much noise as they needed. Tonight, they were rather subdued.

"When I was a kid, I used to love just sitting on our deck and listening to the waves, and sometimes stare up at the stars."

Jesse craned his neck to see beyond the edges of the upper deck. "No stars tonight."

"No. It's cloudy. I'm hoping the winter storm holds off for a bit, or changes course."

The weather predicted a drop of cooler temperatures with flurries. As it was, the year had been unusually strange as the island rarely got snow, and yet this year, it had already exceeded its yearly amount.

The tranquil ebb and flow of the waves filled the air between us, as did the occasional clinking of a wine glass settling on the solid wooden arm.

"It's very soothing. I've missed this." I crossed my legs and relaxed into the chair.

For the past two months, my life had been filled with endless work projects, fighting with Charlie over insignificant items neither of us wanted, but we weren't willing to give the other either, and packing. I needed more nights like this to unwind.

The waves rolled and thundered in a nice rhythmic pattern. In and out. Each breaking wave chipped away at my hardened soul. It wouldn't take much convincing for me to spend the night outside. If it were warmer. As it was, I huddled under the blanket when a cool breeze blew in.

"You know if you want, you can go in and watch a movie. Please don't let me stop you."

"I won't." He propped a foot on his knee. "Like I said earlier, I don't get much company and as quiet as this is, you and I sitting on the deck, it is very peaceful. It's nice."

On the arm rest, his hand twitched, almost like mine was. Desperately, I wanted to hold his hand as it felt like this moment needed it, and with every moving inch of Jesse's hand toward me, I couldn't help but wonder if that's what he wanted too? Even the occasional butterfly took flight, which was strange because I'd long thought they'd died.

The chair shifted beneath Jesse. "I'm just going to ask flat out as I've been debating, and figure to hell with it."

I wrapped my fingers around the base of my wine glass and held on tight.

"Why don't you enjoy Christmas? Are you Jewish?"

The red wine tasted even better than before as I tipped the glass and dumped the liquid into my mouth. I allowed the sweet berry taste to settle before I answered.

"No. I just don't like the holiday, but I won't stop anyone else from celebrating it the way they choose." Suddenly on the defensive, I needed to point out the obvious. "I love that you have lights and decorations all over, and even a set of Christmas lights hanging on your truck, but it's just not something I do."

"You haven't even said 'Merry Christmas'."

I shrugged. "They're just words. No one really means it anyway."

"Most do." He took another sip of wine. "So, if I was to show up at your place, there'd be no colourful lights?"

This year, it was just me and myself, so no decorations at all. One battle we didn't fight was over who got the boxes of decorations, even though there was only a box or two as he kept it to a minimum for my sake. His office however, it was like he was the King of Christmas. His work surface was barely visible over the decorations and dancing Santas and numerous mini trees. I shook my head.

"No trees even?"

I let the silence answer.

"What about presents?"

A smile teased on the edge of my lips and leaked into my words. "Well, those I buy. I have a trunk full for Lily and Eric and Henry. And I left gifts for my friends back home."

I wasn't a complete Grinch, I enjoyed shopping for the perfect present. But I did the same for birthdays and anniversaries. Just because it was the most commercial time of the year, didn't mean I went overboard.

Jesse leaned backed, an expression of satisfaction on his face. "Well, that's good. And are you opposed to receiving gifts?"

It didn't make me super uncomfortable, but I'd rather people save their money than spend it on me. There were other more important things to buy.

"I'm *mostly* okay with it."

"Mostly?" He laughed and swallowed a sip of wine. "My ex-wife loved receiving gifts – the more the merrier, in her opinion. You not liking receiving them, well, that's a first." He chased his head shaking with another gulp of red. "Any particular reason then for not celebrating the holiday? I'm sorry to be asking, I've just never met anyone who didn't like Christmas, and I'm genuinely curious."

But I couldn't answer. As easy as it had been to share with Jesse all about Lily's past and the tip of the iceberg of my marriage being over, I couldn't share the truly personal details.

"It doesn't matter."

"It sure does."

"Nope. I'm just me. One little person in an ocean of people. Me not enjoying the holiday won't affect anyone."

He cocked an eyebrow. "I beg to differ."

It hit me like a two-ton truck, in a way I didn't expect. He wanted to watch a movie and instead we're out here, so in a way, yeah, I did affect someone. The same had been with Charlie. He went overboard on decorations at work because I couldn't stand them in the house.

"Fine. I'll tell you why, but you're not going to like it."

"Let me be the judge of that."

"You've been warned."

Chapter Eight

twisted in my seat, giving my full attention to the handsome man across from me. "You see, the thing is, back when I was a teenager, Lily was in full rebellion…"

"Yes, I remember you saying how wild she was, and how your dad had to stop watching her to take care of your mom."

"That's right." I pulled the blanket up higher, even though I wasn't cold. The patio heater above was raining down plenty of warmth. "Well, Mom always loved Christmas. Like she could give you a run for your money with decorating. Our house was lit up from one side of the lawn to the other, and every room had a tree in it, even if it was just a little one. But on Christmas morning, there would be an extra little present under the tree in our room. It was always the same – a special ornament she found that spoke to her in some way."

Even in the evening glow, it wasn't hard to miss his smile. "Sounds like your mom and I would've had a lot in common."

"I'm sure you would have." I ran the tip of my finger absently around the rim of my wine glass as I wondered what it would be like. Had she not died, the Christmas traditions would've carried on. "Her final Christmas, she wanted to come here. To the beach house."

A tiny tear ripped across my heart, recalling the way Dad carried her up the steps and over to the couch. She was so frail; it was too much work to do on her own.

"And as sure as we set foot here, Lily was gone."

"She needed to seek comfort in her friends?"

I shrugged, having never seen it that way. "Maybe. Or she just couldn't stand…"

The words wouldn't come out. It had been hard watching my mother deteriorate, especially in the time leading up to college when we knew the end was coming. She insisted I still go away but in those three short months her health declined rapidly. When Dad mentioned it was important to have one last Christmas in her favourite place ever, I would've been a fool to have passed. All these years, I'd always thought Lily had seen it as an invitation to go partying.

"Lily and me shared the upstairs bedroom, and per Mom's instructions, we still had to have a little tree in there. Dad had brought both of ours, and we set them up, knowing full well there wasn't going to be an ornament under the tree, but still, we pretended." A lump formed in the back of my throat. "Christmas Eve we all gathered around the couch watching her favourite movie ever – *It's A Wonderful Life* – when she started gasping for breath."

Jesse moved his chair closer and innocently reached for my

hand, his thumb stroking the top of my knuckles.

"Dad sent Lily, who had, by a stroke of luck, managed to be around for a short spell, to start the car and warm it up, while I called 911 to have them phone ahead to the closest hospital."

Ambulance service in a small town was pretty much nil, and the nearest hospital was still an hour away.

"After I hung up, I drove to Spirit Bay as fast as I could, while Dad cuddled in the backseat with Mom. Lily sat beside me, texting like we were going out for pizza or something." I didn't mean for my words to be laced with anger, but yet, after all this time, there it was.

Jesse readjusted the blanket on my lap when I pulled my legs tighter.

"Dad's sobs from the backseat were really hard to ignore, so I broke all the laws racing her to the hospital. But I wasn't fast enough. When we got there, the doctors and nurses put her on a stretcher, but she was already gone. She'd died in Dad's embrace."

Tears trickled down my cheeks, and I was grateful we were sitting in the dark so Jesse wouldn't notice.

Deep down, Mom died the way she wanted. She hated hospitals and clinics but had always enjoyed being snuggled into her true love's arms.

I swiped my hand across my face.

"Lily stayed in the waiting room, fingers tapping a mile a minute on her precious phone, while Dad zoned out. It was days before he truly talked again." I shook my head at the recall.

He was catatonic, unable to eat or drink much.

"The calendar had flipped into a new date by time we got back to the beach house, but no one was in the mood to celebrate Christmas. Dad seemed incapable of making any decisions, so I was completely thrust into charge. We packed our things, and I drove through the night to get us back to our house."

"You did all that?"

"I had too. We just left the house as it was. Decorations up, food in the fridge, you name it."

"Wow. I'm so sorry. I really am. It all makes sense now."

Tears continued down my cheeks. For years, I hadn't told anyone the events of that night. Charlie knew of course, he was my husband, and I needed him to understand why I didn't like Christmas, but other than that?

"Thank you. Thank you for being so kind, Jesse."

The funny thing was the next morning when I woke on Christmas Day from a brief nap after mom's passing, underneath the tiny tree in my bedroom was a little red box just for me, and to this day I've never opened it. The gift goes with me with each move, always unopened. I have no idea who bought it or who put it underneath the tree, and I never will because I refused to open it. For some reason, I even made sure it was packed in my suitcase for this trip.

Jesse continued to hold my hand, rubbing the top in a slow, lazy pass. "You know what I think you need?" He looked into my eyes with a deep and genuine concern. "I think you need a day of fun and relaxation, to just unwind and not dwell on the past. Something to help put a positive spin on the holiday."

I shrugged, not knowing what I needed.

"Aside from breakfast with your sister tomorrow, do you have any plans?"

#

I arrived at breakfast at Lily's the next morning with fresh homemade pastries and cinnamon rolls and other delightful goodies acquired from the local bakery shop. With the box underneath my arm, I rapped my knuckles against Eric's door.

"Oh, Mo, I'm so glad you made it." On Lily's hip was her little boy, Henry. Even tucked into his mom, it was clear how much he'd grown since the last time I'd seen him.

"There he is, my handsome little nephew." I passed the box of goodies over to Eric who stood behind Lily.

Foolishly, I'd hoped Henry would leap into my arms when I extended them, instead he tucked into his mom and hid his face.

"Well, I guess it has been a while."

"Come on in, and meet the gang. Everyone's all here."

Lily walked down the hall, and I followed closely behind. Christmas music played on the stereo and the decorations seemed to have multiplied since when, two days ago? It was crazy.

In the tiny kitchen stood the guests, some I recognized, and some were brand new.

"Hey, everyone, this is my sister, Mona."

The guests quickly went around the room introducing themselves.

There was Beth, Lily's best friend from the city, the interior designer who helped renovate our beach home. She took Henry from Lily and snuggled into him, and an ache formed as I tried not to stare at the easy rapport between them. Guess Beth saw Lily more than I did, and I wasn't sure why that surprised me so much. And hurt too.

There were Cedar and Mitch, each holding a baby. Their five-month-old twins were named Saffron and Ziggy, unique names until I took a good look at Ziggy – his bald little head with a tuft of hair was just like the cartoon character.

Also joining the group, was a blast from the past – Landon Morris. Landon was Eric's big brother; someone I had frequently run into while out hunting for Lily back in the day. Like Eric, he'd undergone the ugly duckling transformation and was a nice-looking man.

He strode over and wrapped me in a hug as if we were old friends. "My goodness, it's been a long time, hasn't it?"

I nodded. "Very much so. You look great."

"Thanks, so do you." His eyes raked over my body.

"She's married, bro, knock it off." Eric clapped his brother on the back and set the box of pastries on the island, opening it to show off the wonderful goodies inside.

"Isn't Mona great? Bought out Sylvia's bakery." My sister smiled and reached for a chocolate turnover at the same time as I did.

Cocking my eyebrow in her direction that at least we still had a few things in common, I had a bite and listened to the others share their stories and laughter, most of which were holiday focused. Conversations revolved around Christmas plans and the general excitement for the impending nuptials tomorrow.

Eric and Lily had set the wedding time for 4pm to say their vows, with a buffet supper to follow, giving the tightly knit group of people time to celebrate the day with family. And all this time I had thought she didn't care for the festivities.

"How many are coming?" I imagined the guest list wasn't too big. It was a beach wedding on Christmas Day, after all.

She pulled out a paper from a folder, one with the full run down on the caterers and rentals and timings for everything. I'll give credit where credit was due, she was uber organized. My wedding day, I was frantic with worry about all the things that could go wrong but with her own wedding, Lily was ready to shrug them off. I envied that ease.

She tapped the list. "With Jesse now coming, thirty-three."

"Jesse's coming?" Cedar asked. "That's great. Maybe he'll meet someone tomorrow, then he won't be so lonely."

Mitch laughed and whipped a cinnamon bun out of the box. "As in meet someone who he doesn't already know?"

"Well, it could happen. Christmas miracles and all that." Cedar took a nibble from a muffin. "I'm glad he's coming. He's such a great guy."

I nodded, trying to contain a smile as I couldn't disagree with her. "I'm staying at his place while our old house gets repaired, and Lily thought it would be a nice thank you to invite him."

Cedar faced Lily. "What's wrong with the house?"

"Broken furnace."

"You should've told me. Mona could've stayed with us. We have an extra room."

I licked my lips, enjoying the heavenly taste of fine chocolate. Somehow, with twins, I suspected there would be even less room at her place than there was at my sister's.

She dismissed the conversation with a wave as the baby in her arms began to wail. "Excuse me, I think she's hungry."

Without a care in the world, she walked over to the couch and lifted her top, nursing her baby as if no one were around.

Landon turned his head away and started making small talk with his brother.

Beth made her way over and sat beside Cedar, asking far too many personal questions about the breastfeeding process. She ended with how excited she was to be trying for baby after her upcoming spring wedding.

I was surrounded by babies and happiness, and while I was thrilled for everyone, the green-eyed monster was rearing its ugly head. They all had what I wanted, and it was really hard to not be jealous because it was no longer in the cards for me. No husband, and thanks to an inhospitable uterus, blocked tubes, and the malfunctioning ovaries of a fifty-year woman, not the thirty-three I was, there'd never be any baby either.

The only thing keeping my tongue at bay was the constant biting of it and thinking about all Jesse and I had shared yesterday.

After our honest conversation last evening, a burden had been lifted from my soul that I couldn't explain. When I woke up this morning, I felt a little happier and although it was Christmas Eve, the lingering sadness had softened a touch. Deep down I knew it was because I had opened up and shared with Jesse, and that in itself was a blessing. There was an unexplainable connection to him, an easiness and naturalness.

Jesse said when my time was done with Lily and Eric to come back to the house and we would go out and enjoy some worry-free, Cheshire Bay excitement. When prompted to explain what he had planned, Jesse said it was a surprise. Then he added it would be something fun and hopefully something that would give me a reason to look back on Christmas Eve with a smile rather than sadness.

Until that time came, my focus was around the revolving conversations about the wedding. It was clear Lily and Eric had planned for everything. Based on all the prep and ideas and vision Lily had for her dream day, it sounded like the most beautifully detailed and perfect wedding, and I was ecstatic how she'd chosen the strip of beach where she'd spend her summers, rather than the standard church, like I had.

More talk about the wedding, and the more I pictured my own second wedding, perhaps someday, maybe. My wedding to Charlie had been a big, big deal. We booked the biggest church in town and filled it with over 250 guests. We rented the largest ballroom downtown and had the best caterers. Our wedding cake was four tiers tall with stairs off to the side, landing on another layer of cake. I suppose in hindsight, the massive production was completely unnecessary. If I had to do it over again, I would do exactly what Lily was doing— a beach wedding was absolutely perfect, and truly, it suited her.

The box of pastries disappeared, the coffee pot had been refilled twice, but everyone was confident in their roles in the wedding. Basically, all we had to do was show up and smile. Everything else would ebb and flow like the waves on the beach.

As Eric put it, "Just enjoy the show."

There wasn't anything else to do really. Beth was the Maid of Honour and Mitch the Best Man, and they'd need to sign a couple of things, but other than that, it was planned to be a stress-free day. Definitely a different way to spend the holiday, but maybe that would be okay too.

The small group broke up, and Lily walked me to the front door as much as I enjoyed the company, I was anxious to leave. It was a constant reminder of all I'd lost, and try as I did, jealousy wasn't a colour I wanted anyone to see me wearing.

"You know, you are more than welcome to hang out with us today." She leaned against the doorframe, arms crossed over her chest, a sweet expression on her face. "We'll have some Christmas cheer and wait for the fat man to dance his way down the chimney."

I rolled my eyes as I pushed into the sleeves of my jacket.

"It doesn't need to be all doom and gloom."

I inhaled sharply and looked beyond her to confirm we were alone. "I am not all doom and gloom."

"Mo, I watched you staring at Cedar as she nursed."

"Yeah, well." My face burned from the rapid induction of heat and I stepped outside, hoping the cool air would work its way across my cheeks.

"It'll happen for you. You and Charlie, you're the perfect couple. It's meant to happen." She brushed her fingers through her blonde tresses. "You'll get pregnant soon."

If she only knew. My mouth opened, and I wanted the words to fall out, but something blocked them from exiting.

"I'm trying to change this holiday, Mo. Make it better."

Slowly, I backed up to the edge of the landing and put my foot down on the first stair, unable to form coherent sentences.

"I miss her too."

I searched my sister's face, looking for any hint of truth in her words. With Lily, she'd never held back, and the earnestness was evident in her voice. Mine, however, laid open raw and exposed. "Do you? Do you really?"

She shrugged and the weight of the world sagged her shoulders. "Some of us chose to move on with our lives, and not let it be the major factor in deciding what to do or how to celebrate. Mom wouldn't want you moping and whining this way. Mom would want you out there living your best life, and you know it to be true."

I half expected her to walk back in the house and slam the door, instead, she stood there with an empathetic grin on her face; maybe becoming a mother herself totally changed her outlook on life. My chin tucked into my chest as my hair fell like curtains on my cheeks. I had no response.

Instead of giving her a witty comeback, or smart assed come back, I simply nodded until the right words formed. "Maybe you're right."

"I love you, Mona."

"And I love you too, Lily." I stepped off the stairs and stood on the sidewalk looking up my little sister.

There was so much I wanted to tell her, so much I wanted to explain, but this wasn't the place, so with a quick little wave I took off and headed back to Jesse's.

Chapter Nine

ily's words echoed through my head, pushing me to Jesse's faster and faster. I ran up the stairs and knocked before I entered.

"How was the day before wedding breakfast?" Jesse sat on the stool at the island, peeling another mandarin.

"It was good."

"Did you tell her about what dissolved between you and your ex?"

"I wanted to." I reached for an orange as the citrusy scent was too hard to pass up. "But no. It's too big to dump on her just yet."

Jesse rose and tossed his peel into the trash. "Eat up. We have some places to visit."

He popped the remaining pieces into his mouth and chewed.

I dumped my single peel into the tissue paper, and pulled apart the orange into its segments, eating one at a time. "What's the plan?"

"You'll see." There was a twinkle in his eye. "But nothing

that hurts, as I know you have a big day tomorrow." He winked for good measure. "How long has it been since you've been here for Christmas?"

"Just that one year."

His head bobbed, and he gave his chin a thoughtful rub. "That's what I suspected. So, you've never really been here in the wintertime?"

I shook my head, little pangs of nervous energy building deep inside. However, I was more curious than scared, excited to see what was planned. I popped the last segment into my mouth. "Ready."

"Wear a warm jacket and mitts."

We were going to be outside, which was fine by me. The sun was starting to peek out from behind the clouds and with the heat, the nip in the air was long gone.

"Let's go." Jesse put on his baseball cap and woolly jean jacket, the keys to his truck jingling from his fingers.

After a quick drive, we were parked at the base of Roden Fields, a panoramic hillside with an impressive view of the airport. Normally, it only snowed for a couple of days in the Cheshire Bay area, but this year, Mother Nature had been unusually cold: a bonus for the residents scattered up and down the hill with toboggans.

"Are we going sledding?" I wasn't sure I was adequately prepared for this kind of outing.

"No objections?" He pulled on his thick gloves and adjusted his jacket.

None to mention, except… "Isn't this for kids?"

"It's for the young at heart." He gave a weak shrug. "Could be for any age really."

Without another word, he exited his truck and I hopped out too, scanning the area to see if we were in fact the oldest ones here. We were not. The laughter and squeals filled the air as dads, it was mostly dads, rode down the hill with a younger child in front. I had to double check as I was sure an old man of a grandfatherly age was slipping down the hill on a saucer, his smile wider than the sheet of plastic separating him from the ground.

"Unbelievable." My words fell out as whisper. However, I couldn't make myself move. It looked fun, and yet, they were all moving so fast.

"It's more fun participating than actually watching." A charming smile spread across his face as he stood beside me.

I inhaled the crisp air and stared into his dark brown eyes. I wasn't a coward and could do this, even if I had to force myself a little. "Fine, let's do it."

We grabbed an old-fashioned wooden toboggan, complete with the curved front, rope handles, and a plaid blanket to give our butts a bit of a cushion. Standing at the top of the hill, slightly breathless from the long climb, we looked down, the incline was much steeper than I expected.

"Are you ready?" Jesse dropped the sled onto the snow and set the blanket upon it.

"You go ahead."

He shook his head. "Ladies first."

I settled myself on the blanket. My feet went on top of the curved part, and then under and finally off to the side. How was this fun?

Tossing my gaze to my left, I spied a dad on a saucer and mimicked his posture – I crossed my feet under me like I'd seen him do.

Jesse hunched down beside me. "Have you never done this?"

The idea of seeing pity on his face was too much to bear, so I instead stared at the frayed yellow rope.

"Really?"

"There were no nearby hills, but I can skate and ski, so all winter activities are not out of the question." I planted a weak grin as I lifted my head and looked over his shoulder, watching in amazement as fearless kids ran and launched themselves onto their boards, flying down the hill without a care in the world.

"You're cute, you know."

My focus adjusted; I could've stayed there forever locked onto those eyes, and my heart skipped a beat as I stared.

"Maybe I should join you, and show you the ropes?" Beneath his toque, an eyebrow rose, and a low chuckle filled the space between us.

Before I could answer, Jesse huddled in behind me, his boots digging into the snow to hold us in place. "Your feet need to go under that."

He pointed to the curved part, but my mind was focused on the firm wall behind my back. Our bodies were pressed together, and it felt so natural. There was zero weirdness.

"What about your feet?" I playfully rolled against him.

"Well, I can put them over your legs…" He demonstrated with his left, keeping the right firmly cemented. "Like this. Or I can hold them up."

"Whatever you think is best, but I'm okay if you drape them over mine. It'll keep me from flying off." The smile I tried to hide leaked out when I braced my hand on his thigh as he wrapped his legs around mine, knees bent as the soles of his boots pushed against the curved front of the toboggan.

"Will do. Ready for a little adventure?"

My skin tingled with anticipation and his strong chest pushed into my back, keeping it warm and comfortable. It was fleeting, but enough to make my breath hitch in my throat. How long had it been since I purposely snuggled into someone?

"Hold on tight."

He rocked us forward and suddenly I was glued into his chest, wind nipping at my exposed cheeks and my hair flapping behind me. My stomach shifted as the ground blurred on the sides and once roaming butterflies were now thrust into my spine.

Still, it was exhilarating, and a small squeal of delight escaped my tightly clenched lips.

Jesse pulled on the ropes, and we glided over to a small shack, coming to a full stop.

Brushing my hair away, he whispered, "How was that?" His words tickled and warmed my ears.

I twisted as much as I could to face him. "The best ride of my life."

My gaze floated down from his warm eyes, over his rugged nose, and settled back on his perfect lips. They were slightly parted and begged me to make the first move with each pulse.

What was wrong with me? It was only a toboggan ride, and he was only asking to be nice, because he was Jesse, sweetheart extraordinaire. After another quick search of his face, I allowed a smile to spread like the sun peeking out from behind a cloud. I patted his arm.

The adrenaline rush was intoxicating, and for now, it was all I was going to get. "Want to do that again?"

Chapter Ten

esse and I walked to the shack after a few more rides down the hill, one of which was completely by myself and ultra scary as I didn't really know how to work the ropes and steer. Thankfully, I only missed a high-end sports car by falling off and holding tight to the ropes so the toboggan wouldn't crash into it.

After that spectacle, he decided it was time for a warm drink around a firepit. It was safer that way.

With a hot chocolate in hand, we found a vacant picnic table and had a seat facing the hill.

"That was fun." I clinked the edge of my plastic lid against Jesse's, the butterflies still swirled and made me feel alive. "Thanks for bringing me here."

"It was my pleasure, mostly." He nudged me. "Next time, I'll bring ear plugs."

"Sorry." I tipped my chin down and mocked a pout.

The screams had been completely instinctual when we

accidently launched over a small bump and got, what I felt, was some serious airtime.

His shoulder touched mine and didn't move away.

"Never hold back with me. Feel free to be yourself. There's only one of you so why hide it?"

"Wise words."

"They only come out after a surge of adrenaline."

"Afraid were you?"

He didn't seem at all like he was scared. In fact, he owned that sled.

He took a sip, and a lingering taste of hot chocolate hung on his upper lip. "Only recently."

It was said so low, I wasn't sure I'd heard correctly. But if I did, what did he mean by that?

His hand rested on his thigh, moving at a snail's pace closer to mine. Was Jesse afraid of what I was believing was growing between us? Was he feeling what I was feeling too? In my heart I wanted to believe love wasn't over, and at my age, there was still a chance I could find happiness with someone who understood me. Could he sense that? Or was I reading way too much into things again? That sounded more likely.

We sat listening to the kids squealing down the hill. It was a first for me to share space with someone and not have the silence breached.

Either we were both comfortable in it, or neither of us knew what to say, and I didn't know Jesse well enough to make an educated guess.

The takeaway cups emptied, and the sun started to lower as a chill settled in the air.

"Shall we move on to the next activity?" He rose and stretched out his legs, taking my empty cup.

"There's more?" I stood beside him, my curiosity more than piqued.

"Always." In a perfect five-point shot complete with a little jump, he landed both in the garbage. "Are you up for it? It's a little more Christmasy than this, but it's something I've done every year since I moved here."

I nodded, pleased with the side effects from the first activity. "Sure."

"You'll have to wear something for me though."

My head tipped to the side, and I scanned his face. What exactly would I have to wear? "Maybe?"

"Maybe? I'll need a yes before we can go." He stood there, digging his boots into the snow, a small smile threatening to spread across his charming face.

"It's pain free?"

"Have I done anything yet that hurts?"

"Well," I paused and pursed my lips together. "There was that fall yesterday at the rink, and today, I just about hit a parked car."

"Those were all on you." He walked close enough to smell

the hint of mint from his hot chocolate.

"But you took me to them?" I had to counter, even if I was only joking.

Jesse rubbed his chin. "True, but…" His hand fell away. "I promise, this shouldn't hurt. It should only make your heart grow two sizes."

I bridged the distance between us, which wasn't much anymore. "Colour me intrigued. With that kind of description, I'll wear whatever you want."

A desire sparked in the depths of his doe-eyed browns, a deep longing of desire. "Let's go."

We drove from the hillside back into Cheshire Bay, and right into the heart of downtown. If you could call it that. More like a cluster of buildings all tucked off the main drag.

However, none of the names on the building were familiar.

"Where are we?"

"The real estate office." He deadpanned comically.

Of course, there was the office of Brunner and Fox. We were parked in front of their main door.

Jesse grabbed the bag nestled between us and pulled out a Santa hat, handing it to me. "You can wear this."

A slight chuckle rumbled out. A hat hadn't been what I'd been thinking I'd have to wear, but I nonetheless pulled off my toque and slipped on the white fur lined hat.

"Done."

"You look cute, and if I had a cape, I'd put it on you so you would be super cute."

Where did he come up with these? Still, a smile stretched across my face at the words and a warm glow settled over my chest. "What will I be doing with this Santa hat on?"

"Aside from being adorable?"

Heat seared my cheeks. "Yeah."

"Well, we're going to go in there..." He pointed to the real estate office, where two people emerged also wearing Santa hats and carrying a few garbage bags.

"And do what?"

"You'll see." Replacing his toque with his Santa hat, he hopped out with a jump and walked over to my side. "This is the best part of the season, for me at least. C'mon."

His excitement was contagious, and I matched him step for step as we went inside.

A few minutes later, he dropped seven bags into the box of his truck.

"You got the addresses?"

"Loading them into my phone now."

They were all in Cheshire Bay. The organization was called A Grinch-less Christmas, a non-profit that collected toys and books for children and delivered them on Christmas Eve by Santa-hat wearing volunteers – Jesse and I being one of dozens of drivers.

CHRISTMAS in CHESHIRE BAY

"There's really this many families without this year?" I was stunned and had expected it in the big city, not in the tiny seaside village.

"Sadly, yes. And most you wouldn't know were broke. Outside appearances and all."

We drove to the first address, a ramshackle walk up fifty years behind in renovations with deep cracks in the sidewalks and along the edge of the foundation. The paint on the wood peeled in long, weathered strips, and the windows had a film on them from years of neglectful cleaning.

After pressing the buzzer and not hearing a response, Jesse tested the door. It pulled open with a creak, but it was a little scary how unsecure the building was. Wasn't that against a landlord/tenant act or something? We climbed the stairs to the third floor and down the dank and dreary hall, still adorned with original 1970's maroon industrial carpeting and faded golden wall sconces.

Since this was my first ever delivery, I stepped to the side and let Jesse knock.

He kept his voice low enough to be heard by the residents on the other side of the door, and not loud enough to echo down the halls. "Delivery for the Akoo family from *A Grinch-less Christmas*."

The walls were paper thin as the song Jingle Bells was being sung on the other side.

The chain slid off, and the door inched opened to a mom of my age holding a child about Henry's age on her hip, who was dressed only in a diaper but waving at us. The lady's sweater dangled off a bone-thin shoulder and her leggings didn't even stretch out the fabric. Bags and dark circles had settled in beneath her eyes but her smile at seeing us was as wide as the Grand Canyon.

Jesse quickly set the bag inside the doorway and stepped back out into the hallway. "Merry Christmas."

The woman's brown eyes filled with tears, and she turned to set her son down. Without warning, she walked to Jesse and wrapped him in a bear hug, planting a kiss on his cheek. "May God bless you, my brother."

He didn't say a word, but the little boy did. "Bess ewe." A cherubic smile filled his face.

She broke from Jesse and before I had the chance to put distance between us, her arms were wrapped around me. There was no mass to her but the strength she exuded was incredible. "God bless you, my sister." A kiss also graced my cheek.

"Bess ewe," the little boy echoed from the safety of the kitchen as he waved with delight.

I swallowed down a lump rapidly forming in my throat, but words failed to release.

She retreated into her home, twisting her hands. "Do you know if the food bins are coming?" Her face contorted into an apologetic expression, as if she had no right to ask.

Jesse glanced at his watch. "They haven't come by yet?"

The woman shook her head and lowered her gaze.

He reached into his wallet and retrieved a twenty, leaving the billfold empty. "I know it's not much, but this should help until they arrive. Donnelly's is open until nine."

Jesse didn't have money to spare. Not after our conversations.

I reached into my purse and added a couple of twenties to his.

"Oh no, I can not accept. The food bins will be here. I believe." Her hand covered her heart.

"Please." I took the money from Jesse's outstretched hand and thrust it into hers, quickly glancing into her apartment.

There were no toys on the floor, and there was only one couch, covered in a sheet with a pillow on the far end. A scuffed table with two mismatched chairs added to the furniture, but that was all. Whatever hard times befell on this poor woman; she was barely scrapping by.

Her hands trembled as she looked us in the eyes. "God bless you both. Merry Christmas."

My own tears formed, and I tried hard to blink them back into their holds. Breaking the eye contact, I nodded and walked away, the words *Merry Christmas* dancing in my head but unable to find a way out.

I rested my fur-covered forehead against the cool of his truck, fighting to hold myself together while my breath lodged itself in the back of my throat.

Jesse caught up to me. "Hey, you okay?"

I kept my back to him and pulled myself further into my jacket. "I'm fine."

His hand settled between my shoulder blades. "I honestly didn't expect that kind of a reaction from you."

Firm hands on my shoulders, he turned me around, and I buried my face into him.

"They are so…" The words refused to leave my lips.

"Yes, that's true, but the best part is, they are grateful for everything they have, and take nothing for granted." In a soothing motion, he rubbed my back, all the while whispering in my ear. "There's more to life than materialistic things. We can be grateful for the sun and fresh air, and for friends and love. For the song she was singing."

"But you also need the other things."

"Sure, her living conditions aren't ideal, but she's out of the weather. The food bins will make sure she has the necessities. But I'm absolutely positive of one thing."

I looked at Jesse through my blurred vision. "What's that?"

"I bet she loves her baby more than anything on Earth and goes out of her way to make sure he's taken care of."

I had to agree. The baby didn't appear to be suffering. He was bright and happy, full of life.

Jesse brushed his lips across my forehead, and I wished he had tried about four inches lower, even if this wasn't the right moment. "Do you want to come with me for the other deliveries?"

"Are you kidding?" I wiped away my tears and smiled at the incredible man standing before me. "I'm knocking first."

Chapter Eleven

The last delivery completed, we sat in his truck, the emotional exhaustion tugged on my heartstrings.

"Do you feel up for one more activity?"

Deep down, I was tuckered out and debated saying no, but it was Jesse. So far everything he suggested had been fun, if not a bit life changing.

"What did you have in mind?"

"It's not a long activity, but it comes with food, drinks, and a healthy dose of Christmas cheer."

"Hmm." My stomach rumbled at the thought of a bite to eat, and my mouth was a little dry too. "Sure. Should I keep the Santa hat on?"

"Yeah." A large grin parked on his face, refusing to move. "You look cute in it."

"Thanks." My cheeks heated and my body thrummed from the compliment. "And thanks... For today."

"Thanks for tagging along. It was nice having someone join me for this."

I sat up straighter. "Your ex-wife never came with you?"

"Not once." The truck rumbled to life, and he put it into gear.

"Well, she truly missed out. I want to do this next year."

Although it wasn't me doing the giving as all the toys had been donated, it warmed my heart to be a part of this experience. To see the smiles on stranger's faces and the light in their eyes. If only for a little bit, these deliveries eased a bit of burden and helped the families believe in the magic of Christmas.

If Mom were around and knew about this, I could imagine her going from place to place, likely toting a wrapped package of homemade goodies to add to each delivery and inviting them over for dinner. Yeah, Mom would've loved this.

"Come back next year and it's a date."

A date. A future date. With Jesse. Even if it was a year from now, I wasn't going to forget. Guess my next Christmas was already planned.

The ride to wherever this final activity was went by quickly, and before I knew it, we were back at the skating rink. "Didn't we do this activity yesterday?"

However, the area was different. Food trucks were in abundance around the edges of the rink and at the far side, a small bonfire was lit. But what caught my eye most of all was the giant tree in the centre of the field.

"It's the tree lighting ceremony tonight."

"Let me guess? *You* never miss it." I kept my tone playful. No doubt, based on everything else I'd learned about Jesse, he'd be all over this activity.

"Not once." He tipped his head to the side, the pom-pom from his Santa hat rubbing against his cheek. "Come on, let's check it out, but I'm hungry, you?"

"Yeah." In fact, my stomach rumbled at the thought. "Anything you'd recommend?"

Slowly, he checked out the five food trucks. "Do you like spicy food?"

My eyes widened. "Absolutely."

"Then I suggest *Mexilente.*" He said it with a straight face, but I didn't hold back my giggle.

Nudging each other like we were old friends, we bumped our way over to the food truck and placed a tomato-free order.

Dinner over, which we both gobbled down without many words spoken, we ambled through the growing crowd. People congregated around the main part of the field where the tree stood as electricians fiddled with a plethora of black cables.

"Do they bring in a tree each year, like Rockefeller Center?"

His brows pinched together. "You don't remember the tree yesterday?"

101

The undecorated, plain-Jane tree had not captured my attention the way the charming man beside me did. Jesse was proving to be unlike any guy I'd ever met, which is horribly cliché, but true.

In high school, I'd started dating Charlie because he gave me the time of day and was interested. But after all those years together, I had finally washed my hands of him. It was time to move on.

"Hey, Jesse?" A ball of nervous energy gathered in the pit of my stomach, and I shoved my hands deep into my pockets.

"Yeah?"

Opening up to another human being had always been a weak spot of mine, and although I'd shared more with Jesse in the past two days than I had with many people, it still unnerved me. I was grateful for his attentiveness and warmth of spirit, and I needed to tell him, but I didn't know how.

"What's on your mind?" He stopped in front of me and brushed away a strand of hair.

I tore my gaze away to the tree twenty feet behind him. We were close enough to see the strings of lights and thousands of golden feet of garland. Somewhere off in the distance, likely on the other side of the tree, carollers sang out.

"Oh look." I tilted my head back as giant snowflakes danced to the ground. "It's so pretty."

"Yes, it is." But he wasn't watching the falling flakes, he was locked onto me.

A warmth spread through my core and radiated out to the tips of my fingers. It had been a long time since I'd seen an expression filled with so much desire. His dark eyes searched right into my soul, and the best part was, it didn't frighten me.

Around us, voices broke through, chanting out a countdown. As the 'one' faded into the background, the tree lit, washed in pinpoints of golden lights, reflecting off the strands of garland and tinsel. A giant star at the top danced as the colours faded from white to gold to silver and back again.

"Oh wow." The sight took my breath away, and I returned my focus back to Jesse. "It's breathtaking. Thank you for bringing me here. Thank you for today. I've really enjoyed myself."

I searched his dark eyes and allowed my gaze to float lower over his nose, across his whiskery cheeks and chin until it settled on his perfect pair of kissable-looking lips. My whole body was on fire and if I didn't make a move soon, I was bound to implode.

"Thank you for being a part of this. I've never had anyone to share it with."

Right, because his ex-wife wasn't into it. The gifts, sure, but the magic of it all? No interest. And really, until a couple of days ago, I had never really experienced the magic of the holiday either. It had been trying to find the perfect gift, ignore the noise, and pretty much treat it as any other day.

However, I was starting to understand the holiday. The fascination with it. The time of year where people gave more of themselves than they ever expected back, if they even expected anything back. People like Jesse, who didn't have two nickels to rub together, and yet delivered toys to underprivileged children and handed out his own money to help a starving mother. Jesse, the guy who didn't need to spend money to have a blast and enjoy life whether it was skating or going tobogganing, and yet, who enjoyed the calm of the evening, listening to the waves from the back deck of his house. Guys like him were one in a million. Or rarer.

My gaze danced over his, and I leaned a little closer, parting my lips in breathless anticipation. I wanted him. To taste him. To feel his arms holding me tight. And as I searched his eyes, I was sure he wanted the same thing.

He inched himself closer, and with his finger, tucked a piece of hair behind my ear. "You're beautiful."

Breathable air was long gone.

"All day long, I've wanted to touch you." His gaze flittered between my eyes. "Am I overstepping? Am I reading too much into this?"

It was the faintest of head shakes to roll out of me, but he accepted my answer and cupped his hand on my cheek, replacing the cool with a burst of heat that radiated across my face and down over my chest.

"You're not." My words were but a faint whisper.

"I want to kiss you. I've been fighting it all day."

"You don't need to fight anymore." Because I wanted him too. I pushed up on the balls of my feet and leveled myself to him, taking in the wanton desire building in his eyes.

Without another word, he brushed his lips across mine, and I wrapped my arms around his neck to pull him in closer and tighter. Jesse's kiss had incredible strength and power as I suddenly felt like I was floating, and we'd been transported to another world. His hands slipped to the small of my back, instantly electrifying me, and I pushed deeper into a kiss I never knew was possible.

The world around us faded out of sight, a blur of twinkling lights, muted carollers, and fuzzy snowflakes wrapping around us. I kissed him and welcomed him into a place long deserted. Kissing Jesse gave me new life and the swirling butterflies in my gut launched themselves, lifting me into the heavens.

"Mona Baker Jones! What the hell is wrong with you?"

That's when I crashed to the ground.

Chapter Twelve

y little sister stormed over to stand in front of me, while Eric pulling Henry on a child's sled slowly caught up.

"What the hell are you doing?" She glared at Jesse. "And you! You should be ashamed of yourself. She's a married woman."

In a move I didn't expect, Jesse tightened his grip around my waist. I expected him to drop and hightail it out of there. I've seen Lily's explosions before; they weren't pretty. She was more like a grenade taking everyone around her out.

"Lil, I think we need to talk." I swallowed down a bite of bile which had risen fairly quickly. Long gone were the flutters of excitement and anticipation, now the adrenaline surging through me was ready for a fight.

Lily glanced back to her fiancé and son. "I'll be right back."

She turned her angry eyes in my direction. Having seen this expression in her many times, mostly when I was dragging her back home, I wasn't too worried. Especially since I'd long given up on my sister actually liking me.

"Let's go."

"Somewhere more private." If I was going to explain the failings in my life, I didn't want witnesses.

She marched over to an area between the skate shack and the tree, no one was in ear shot. "What the hell?"

"Lily, there's something you need to know." I sighed and dug my boot under the snow. Best to spit it out, pick up the pieces, and fill in any blanks. "Charlie and I... We've been having problems."

"So?" Her eyes narrowed, and if I didn't know better, the daggers were being lined up, readying for launch. "That gives you no right to kiss another man. That's adultery."

I nodded, as I didn't disagree.

"The thing is…" I inhaled a sharp bite of cooled air. "Charlie and I split up." Oh my god, I actually said it to her. The relief was overwhelming, and I no longer shouldered the burden of keeping it secret.

The daggers lowered and her voice softened. "What? When?"

"A year ago, last December, just after Christmas. He moved out shortly thereafter and let me stay in the house while it was being listed, until it sold. Three days ago, I moved into my own apartment after signing the divorce papers. It's over."

She stood unmoving like a stone statue, with only her lips forming the barest of syllables. "Divorce?"

"We had to. We couldn't make it work. Charlie always

wanted kids, and well…" I stared at the flakes gathering on Lily's shoulders and arms. "I'm broken, Lily. I can't ever have children."

The words stung like an arrow through the heart. Broken was the only word for it. Not only was my uterus inhospitable, but my ovaries functioned like a person twenty years older. Egg production was sporadic at best with weak to non-existent LH levels. At one appointment well over two years ago, just before things dried up between Charlie and me, my ob-gyn was pretty sure early onset menopause was less than two years away. Sadly, he had been correct.

"But adoption? Or other plans?"

I checked the grounds and spied Jesse standing chatting with Eric. He was looking in my direction.

"It wasn't just that, and it would be easy to say, yeah that's what drove us apart, but it was so much more. We weren't the best versions of ourselves with each other. He didn't make me happy, and I know I didn't make him happy. Sex was a chore, and we both hoped a baby would turn things around for us."

Her eyes blurred, and she stepped closer. "Oh, Mo."

"It's okay. I've come to peace with it." I lifted my shoulders and let them fall with a hearty sigh. "I'm okay being me. Being Mona Baker."

"Why didn't you tell me? Why did I have to find out this way?" There it was – the hurt in her voice at being one of the last to know.

I didn't know how to answer her without inflicting pain.

"We've never been close, you know that. I'm not even your Maid of Honour."

"Are you upset about that?" Her words twisted like her lips as she spoke.

"Honestly? Not at all. Beth deserves the honour." It was true, and never once did I begrudge that. Beth had been Lily's best friend for several years. "Besides, I'm happier being in the background."

"You're not in the background, you're giving me away." She cocked an eyebrow.

"You know what I mean."

But the scrunched nose and questioning eyes said otherwise.

"I'm your biggest pain in the ass and you know it." The words came out with a gust of a laugh.

"Yes, you are." She playfully punched me in the shoulder. "But seriously, if it wasn't for you, I'd likely be dead."

"Well, I don't know about that."

"I do. I know I don't say it much, because it's hard for me, but I really do love you, Mona."

My head tipped to the side unexpectedly. "You do?"

"Why are you so surprised?"

"Because I always believed you hated me."

She had the gall to laugh. "I've never hated you. You were a mini mom for me. When she got sick, you sort of took over."

"It was never my plan."

Jesse turned away to answer a call.

Lily shifted on her boots and tugged at the scarf around her collar. "Maybe not, but I got you away from the sadness that always seems to take up residence. God, it was awful." Her gaze turned up toward the falling snowflakes.

"What?"

"You don't remember? She was sick from the chemo-" She squared her shoulders and stood up to her full height.

"I know what the sadness and sickness was all about. I cleaned it up." More often than I thought was necessary.

"I hated being around that, and I know you did too. I knew if I snuck out, you'd be forced to come and find me, so in a way, I felt as if I was helping you too. It got you out of the house for a bit too."

"It was never fun. Some nights I had to hunt you down for hours."

"But it was hours you weren't spending listening to her throwing up and gagging and whimpering."

It was more than that. "You cost me time with her."

"Really? You *wanted* to sit there with her as she vomited." Her face took on a greenish hue as if recalling the memories soured her own stomach. "No, thank you."

"Don't you regret it?"

"Seeing her that ill?" She planted her foot firmly on the ground and thrust her hands into her pockets. "Not for a single moment. That wasn't Mom. The disease had taken over and killed who she was."

A gasp escaped me and hung in the air between us.

She reached out a hand and squeezed my arm. "I will always remember the good times, and the fun we used to have, but I don't want to remember her when she was at her worst. That's why I was never home. And a good thing too because look at what it did to you." She stabbed me in the chest with a long finger. "You used to be so strong, and strong willed. You never gave up on anything and you fought the good fight. Now, you've walked away from your marriage and given up on having a family..."

I thrust my hand in front of her face. "Stop. You know nothing about my marriage to Charlie. Nothing." My voice rose. "And happiness isn't about just having kids and being in a marriage, it's about finding someone who respects you and cares for you. Look at Mom and Dad; he loved her more than anything else on the planet, and she loved him the same way. Charlie and me? We were never like that, and looking back now, I can see that. It was as if we settled for each other. Charlie wasn't a risk taker, and I wasn't much of a risk."

"Don't talk about yourself that way."

"I was never you. I couldn't go to a party and be this beacon of light and energy, and the popular gal everyone wanted to hang with."

"Were you jealous?"

I nodded, despite my unwillingness to do so. "So much. You were everything I wanted to be."

"Oh wow."

"You got everything you ever wanted."

"As did you."

"No, I didn't." I shook my head and stared in Jesse's direction as he paced back and forth. "But that's okay. I'm working on it. I'm working on being me and, most important, liking me. I'm trying new things, and I'm stepping outside my comfort zone."

"Like being back here?"

"Yeah." A smile leaked from the edges of my lips. "I came here *because* of you. Regardless of what things are like between us, you're still my little sister. I promised Dad I would take care of you."

"Did he know about your issues with Charlie?"

I shook my head. "I've barely told anyone. Work knows, as I had to amend all sorts of paperwork, and well, Jesse knows. It fell out of me the first night here."

"Your marriage is truly over?"

"Well before we split up." I squared my shoulders, the pressure lifted. "Charlie's getting married in the summer."

"No shit!" Lily's eyes widened and she shook her head. "That didn't take long. About Jesse, what's going on with that?" She asked like a little sister would ask a big sister, with wide eyed curiosity, before she flipped her gaze over to where his pacing was picking up speed.

"Not sure yet, but I wouldn't mind finding out."

"What's holding you back?"

"Fear." A burden I'd been carrying around for years shattered all around me as I said the word. "What if I'm not good enough?"

"What if you are?" Her eyes lit up. "Go find out!"

Chapter Thirteen

ily wrapped me in a hug, something I was really starting to enjoy, until she pushed me away with a huge grin pushing up the corners of her eyes.

"What are you waiting for? Go to him."

What was I waiting for?

I had enjoyed that kiss and wanted more from Jesse, but how could we make it work? My home and work were six hours away. That alone should've put the brakes on anything, but yet, it was impossible to deny the connection between us, and the way it continued to grow in strength.

Still, my walk back to him was more of a run as I couldn't wait to be in his arms.

"Hey," I breathed out as soon as I was within kissing distance.

A sadness clouded his features. "I'm sorry. But I have to go."

Damn. I had misjudged the situation and the growing interest between us.

He lifted his phone and repocketed it. "The hospital called. I have work to do."

"Oh." Work to do, code for mortician stuff. On Christmas Eve.

My heart spluttered in my chest as a wave of emotion washed over me. Someone that dreadful night had taken care of Mom.

He ran a finger down my cheek, leaving trails of heat. "Don't do this to yourself, I can see what you're worried about."

What was I worried about? Someone, somewhere, was mourning the loss of a family member. On Christmas Eve. A heartache I was all too familiar with.

"Okay." Smarter words would've been better.

"I need to go, but I can drop you off back home or Eric has offered to have you stay with them. I could be a while."

I inhaled sharply and gazed around. It was amazing to see people carrying on and enjoying the festivities without a care in the world, and here I was, after having the most perfect day and kiss with a sweetheart of a guy, and a reconciliation of sorts with my sister, prepping to send him into the trenches. I wanted the magic to continue. Life wasn't fair.

"You can take me back to your place." I lifted my hand for him, and he grabbed onto it, walking us back over to Lily and Eric, who no doubt, was on the receiving end of Lily's wagging tongue.

Eric gave us his full attention. "So?"

Jesse spoke. "I'm going to take her home."

"Are you sure, Mo?" Lily's face wore sympathy.

"I swear I'm okay. Besides, I have a few gifts to wrap." And maybe, finally, it was time to open the little red box stored in the bottom of my suitcase. "I'll see you in the morning, after you have a full night of beauty sleep."

Lily gave my arm a squeeze. "Easier said than done as I have a toddler who doesn't believe in sleeping through the night." She winked and smiled, tossing a *goodbye* over her shoulder as she walked away.

"I really don't want the day to end like this." Jesse stopped on the passenger side and opened the door. "Not this way."

But I didn't know how to respond. I didn't want the night to end either, and although it was still relatively early, it wasn't even nine yet, it would be in the wee hours of morning before he returned.

The drive back down the lane to Jesse's place was quick, but quiet, and he parked in front of his house. His hand was poised on the ignition as if he were going to turn the truck off.

"You go. I've got a key, remember?" I retrieved it and let it dangle under the glow of the multi-coloured lights hanging in his truck.

"But I…"

I inched my way across the bench seat and stared into his perfect face, leaning in close enough to smell his woodsy scent. "I'll see you later."

"In the morning. Don't wait up." He brushed his lips across

mine, setting a roar of flaming embers alight.

With each breath he stole from me, I became more a part of him. Finally, I pulled back, desperate to continue this inside, but knowing full well someone else needed him. "Go."

"I've never had such a hard time going to work. And I love my job." A sadness settled over him. "I really want to stay."

But I knew he couldn't. As unfortunate as his job was, it helped to pay his bills and he needed the money. To make it easier on him, I inched back to the door and pushed it open.

"See you soon." I blew him a kiss and hopped out.

He put the truck in gear and drove away, the Christmas lights on the box of his truck waving as he disappeared.

Entering Jesse's home, I hung up my jacket and tidied up the place a bit, although Jesse was no slob. I prepped a breakfast of baked French toast and readied it for the oven for when we woke up. It was Mom's old recipe, another Christmas favourite, but I hadn't had it in years.

As I washed and dried the last of the dishes, I stared at the ceiling. Up there was the little red box. The last gift she'd given me.

After finding a bit of Christmas magic today, all thanks to Jesse, it was time to finally open it. I felt that deep in my soul.

I trudged up the stairs and popped the suitcase onto the bed, digging through the depths of the contents to retrieve the hand-sized boxed. The edges of the red ribbon had frayed over the years, but the bow was still intact. My finger outlined the edge of the tag, which had faded, however, the beautiful script Mom was famous for, still spelled out my name.

Somehow, the only place fitting to open it was in front of the tree. I held the box close to my heart as I descended the stairs and made my way back over to the shimmering tree, lighting it up with a touch of a button.

My heart was pounding loudly, and it was nearly impossible to hear myself think over the rush. This was it. Once I opened it, I'd never have another gift from her again, and as I gently tugged on the bow, I stopped.

Maybe this wasn't the right time to open it.

I stared at it in the glow of the Christmas tree.

Perhaps I should add Jesse's gifts under there first?

Holding the little red box, I went back upstairs, got the couple of gifts I'd found, and wrapped them in paper decorated with little snowmen. First, a monthly subscription to a sock of the month club, as I'd noticed his socks were thread bare. I'd also enrolled him in a local treat box for six months, where he'd get a selection of snacks all made on the island. Added to that, were a couple of ornaments from Whimsical Whims and a gift card to Pete's Pitas.

In my nicest handwriting, I penned out his name, although my penmanship needed work. It wasn't nearly as scriptly beautiful as Mom's had been. Still, once they were under the tree, it made it look less bare, and a smile spread across my face.

I sat on the springy couch and wiggled myself into place,

staring at the box on the edge of the coffee table and the tree behind it. Why was I so nervous about undoing the knot and lifting the lid? Never had that problem any other year when it was there. In fact, it was the first gift I opened.

My hand shook as I reached for the box and held it in my hand, admiring it from all sides. Really, I was being ridiculous and the inner child in me undid the knot in a lightning-fast motion, while the hurting, grown adult slammed the brakes. I set the box back down, pushing it into the middle of the table. As much as I thought I was ready, I wasn't. Not really.

Besides, it was Christmas Eve, not Christmas morning, and I only opened presents then. It was a hard and fast rule.

Relieved for having stopped myself from making a mistake, I hopped back into the kitchen and whipped up some muffins; a hearty variety that froze well and would fill Jesse with nutrition in my absence. It also helped to pass the time, and before I knew it, the clock struck twelve.

"It's now Christmas Day," I said to no one, putting the cooled muffins into a freezer-safe container and sliding them into a narrow vacant spot in his freezer.

The lights in the kitchen had just flicked off when a key rattled in the door and grabbed my full attention, cementing my feet to the floor.

Jesse slowly opened the door and stepped inside. Even in the shadows, his face lit when he spotted me. "Oh, hey. You're still up."

"Hey." Was it wrong to ask how work was? Or would that be weird?

"It smells good in here." He lifted his nose to take in the scents.

"Muffins and breakfast for the morning." When he walked over, I pointed out the tray in the fridge, and the snacks in the freezer.

"You didn't have to."

"I didn't mind. Wanted to make sure you had good food to eat when I wasn't around." And like always, I was an A+ mood killer as the smile fell right off his face.

"You didn't need to stay up."

"I was killing time. Remember the Christmas gift my mother left for me the morning she passed away? I started to open it." I pointed to the coffee table where it sat untouched, the ribbon laying around the base.

"You opened it?" There was so much hope in his voice, I hated to disappoint him once again.

"No. But I got further with it than I ever had before, so it's progress," I said with as much conviction as I could muster.

"You were just waiting for me, weren't you?" It came out in a tired giggle as he wrapped his arms around my waist and pulled me close.

Maybe a part of me had been waiting, needing the extra support. However, I pushed him away and wrinkled my nose as there was a strong odor in his clothing.

"Give me five?"

I nodded and he raced upstairs. The shower started, and I allowed my mind to wander into dirty little places I hadn't ventured into for a while. While Jesse cleaned himself, I poured us a couple of glasses of red wine. Was it too late for a little drink? Nah, it was Christmas Eve, or rather, it was now Christmas Day. However, rather than fill to a normal amount, I halved it, just enough for a little toast, and set them on the coffee table.

A fresh Jesse fell in beside me on the couch and reached for his glass, lifting it for me.

I mirrored his action, and the gentle clink filled the air.

He took a sip and licked his lips. "Merry Christmas, Mona."

"Same to you." The words were right there on the tip of my tongue, but I just couldn't let them slip out.

"Are you going to finish opening it?"

I stared at the pretty package. "Not sure." It suddenly felt heavy as I lifted it back into my hands. "Maybe."

"I can leave, if you'd prefer. I didn't want to interrupt."

But I didn't want him to take off. After everything I'd shared with him, it was like he needed to be here when I finally lifted the lid. "No. Stay."

I snuggled into the depths of the couch, and Jesse draped his arms over my shoulders. He smelled good, a sultry spicy scent. Whatever it was, the deeper I inhaled, the calmer I became.

For good measure, I took another sip of wine and swallowed

down the fear. This was it. The last gift. My wine glass wobbled as I set it on the table, and my hand trembled as I pulled off the lid.

Chapter Fourteen

Inside the box, was a tissue-wrapped ornament, but that wasn't what caught my eye. Tucked into the lid was a folded note written on blue paper.

If my hands had been shaking before, that had nothing on what they were doing now. Tropical storms moved things less.

Jesse's hand squeezed my shoulder. "I'll give you a minute."

I put my hand on his pajama-covered leg. "Stay. Please. I insist."

Inhaling, I counted to three before I released my breath and unfolded the note. My eyes fell upon the words *My Dearest Mona* and the tears fell out like a flash flood.

Her beautiful script scrawled out a short message about how I changed her life when I made her a mom; the best thing to have ever happened and she hoped someday when I had a child, I'd understand that kind of undying love. Every day she was proud of me, for giving more of myself than I had to spare, for taking care of

Dad and Lily and her. For finding strength in the darkest of places and still seeing the light on the heaviest of days.

I chuckled through tears as I read, it was typical Mom to mess up the metaphors.

She wished me unending joy and happiness and to find the one who fills my heart with love and desire, the kind of person who you miss instantly when they are out of sight and can't wait to be back in their arms. The kind of contentment that only comes with finding your soulmate and passion.

Her final written words were: *Never settle for less than you deserve, for you deserve the very best.*

"Oh, Mom." My heart ached as the tears continued to rain down my cheeks.

Jess squeezed me tight, and I pulled a touch of his strength to wipe my face with the back of my hand. I folded the note back into place and tenderly unwrapped the tissue paper, pulling out the glass ball. Inside the ornament were rolled pieces of paper, and on the outside was the word *Memories* and the year before my birth until her last year. Had she written all her favourite memories of us throughout the years? There were so many miniature scrolls.

I held it in front of the twinkling tree lights and stared.

Jesse whispered, "She's always with you."

I tipped my head against him and nestled the treasure into the box as a wave of bittersweet peacefulness settled over me. Her words replayed over and over in my mind, until the dawn of the new day broke across the horizon, brightening the living room.

When I awoke, it was clearly morning. Somehow, I was covered in a blanket, and Jesse's lap had been my pillow. As I stretched, I opened my eyes and stared into the sleepy face looking down on me.

"Morning." His voice was groggy and raw, and he cleared the frog away. "How'd you sleep?"

I pushed myself into a sitting position and wiped at the tiny crust of dried drool. The picture of attractiveness. Not wanting to chance breathing dragon's breath onto him, I turned my head and stretched out my neck. "It was good."

Better than good. One of the best night's sleep I've had in ages, but I was sure it wasn't all due to Jesse. Part if it was because the burden was lifted. At least that was my thought.

Standing on my feet, a gust of cool air settled over me once the warm blanket was lifted. I cocked an eyebrow. "You?"

He chuckled, a sweet sound I wanted to always hear. "I believe I did."

My gaze scanned the room, settling on the base of the tree. The presents had multiplied at some point during the night.

"Merry Christmas." Jesse stood beside me.

"That was a first for me, as an adult."

"What was?"

"Sleeping in front of the tree like that. It was kind of pretty."

Lights all twinkling, the rhythmic noise of a spinning ornament, the gentle crest of waves beating on the shoreline and another body to keep me warm and secure. Seriously, a person could get used to spending the holidays here.

Jesse touched the tip of my nose with his finger and then curled it and gently lifted my chin up to gaze into my eyes. "I'll admit, I haven't done that either. That's a first."

"We're really quite the pair, aren't we?" My eyes danced between his, and my gaze lowered over his perfect cheeks and settled on his kissable lips.

His ex-wife was crazy for not sticking around. He was a keeper. If only there wasn't a whole cross-island distance between us, we could continue to explore this growing connection, rather than have it severed in two days time. I was due home, back to work on the twenty-eighth, back to whatever life I was willing to let myself live.

He tipped his head to the side and moved in closer, our chests fusing with each whisper of a kiss until neither could stand the anticipation further, and we gave into the pull. The kiss was hot enough to melt icebergs, and I desperately wanted to explore more, however, movement out on the beach caught my eye, and I yanked away in surprise.

"The wedding." It rolled off my tongue like it had been something I'd forgotten about, which couldn't have been further from the truth.

Jesse walked to the back door and hung his hands from the door frame, stretching out his back. "Looks like they are setting up chairs and the wedding arch thing."

"Maybe I should throw breakfast in and go clean myself up?"

"Breakfast would be a great idea. Maybe I'll toss it in for you, if you tell me what it needs to cook at?" He stepped over and once again held me tight.

It didn't get old, and unlike with Charlie, whose hold I couldn't wait to get out of, I found myself missing Jesse the moment we broke apart. It was the weirdest feeling. But I needed a shower and a good teeth scrubbing.

"Unwrap and bake at 350 for 30 minutes." I was already halfway down the hall.

"I'm on it." The oven beeped as he punched in the temperature.

Without another word, I headed up to the shower, and had myself a little quickie cleaning. The warm scent of cinnamon and a pot of freshly brewed coffee filled my senses as I strutted back into the kitchen in my button up blouse and blue jeans, with my prettiest underwear on beneath. Had I known I could be something unwrapped, I would've packed something nicer.

Jesse folded the newspaper and hopped off the stool, his gaze raking me over and warming me up nicely. "I know the invitation said business casual, but are you wearing that to the wedding? I think your sister would have a bird."

Yep, Lily would go hog wild. "I'll be changing after I do my hair and makeup. This way, if I spill, I'm not getting it on my dress."

"The rollers really add to the look." He tapped one for good measure.

For some reason, I didn't feel the need to hide in my room as my hair set. "I'd thought I'd go with sexy beach wave hair."

"You could go dressed exactly as you are, and you'd still be the prettiest one there."

A building heat flashed across my chest and flooded my neck and cheeks. "Stop," I whispered.

"I'm sorry. Am I making you uncomfortable?"

My gaze fell to the timer on the stove. Three minutes remained; however, the island was already set for two.

"Didn't your husband compliment you?"

"Of course, it's just…" Been a while. Compliments became special occasion words, or when Charlie was really horny and hoped to turn me on for a reason other than a baby-making romp in the hay. And that was well over eighteen months ago.

"It's unfortunate. For him, I mean."

My heart skipped a beat, and I slowly made eye contact.

"Because I get to be the lucky one who tells you how amazing and beautiful you are. And I'll try to say it as often as I can until you believe it for yourself."

I had so many questions for him, and so few possible answers. The biggest was where this was going. Or where could he see it going, as I was starting to believe I wasn't just seeing what I'd hoped to see. Would a long-distance relationship be something doable?

I didn't know, having never been in one. Charlie had been my one and only serious boyfriend, so I really had much to learn about being in a relationship. Things had changed since I'd last dated. What if I screwed up?

The oven beeped, and Jesse headed over to remove breakfast and set it on the hot mats between our plates.

My gaze fell to the folded newspaper, still surprised the Island Gazette still published. "How often do you get the paper?"

"Sundays."

"That's it?"

"Not much goes on here."

Which I supposed was true. I opened the paper and flipped through, wondering if I'd stumble upon wedding news. Nothing. However, the job section caught my eye. Bauer Mechanical was looking for a cost accountant to oversee their west coast operations on Stewart Sound, which covered Cheshire Bay.

At this point in my life, I had nothing to lose. My rental was a month-by-month situation, and my job? I wasn't loyal to it and had no close friends or buddies there. It was definite food for thought.

For now, I sat on the stool across from the man who made my butterflies swarm and my heart beat double time, and served him a healthy, man-sized serving of baked French toast. As he poured the sticky syrup over his slices, his phone buzzed, and he tugged it out of his pocket.

"I need to take this, sorry." Without explanation, he hopped off his stool and skedaddled down the hall. "Hey, honey," he said in a soft tone as he bounded up the stairs.

Chapter Fifteen

Who was Jesse talking to? And more importantly, why did he scamper off and disappear when the call came in?

While I waited for him to return, I finished a thick slice of French toast and peeled an orange. I'd even managed to top up my coffee and add a drizzle of milk to it.

Finally, Jesse made his way back into the kitchen, a satisfied smile on his face. He cut into his breakfast and popped a piece into his mouth, chewing slowly and letting a deep moan escape. "This is very tasty."

"I'll leave the recipe for you." My voice was curt, surprising me as the tone rolled out.

Yes, I was having feelings for Jesse, and judging by the way he kissed me, he was too, so the *hey honey* phone call really rubbed me the wrong way.

"You okay?"

I took a sip of coffee and held back from slamming it on the tabletop. "I'm going to be honest. I really enjoy your company."

He reached beyond the fruit basket and held my hand. "And I enjoy yours. These last couple of days have been amazing."

"They have been, yes." It was hard to disagree. "Which makes things difficult."

"How so?"

"I'm going home in two days."

"So?" He stabbed another piece and popped it into his mouth.

I ripped the orange peel into tiny fragments, unsure of where I was taking this conversation. Or even what the end result would be. "I've shared more with you than I have anyone else in a long time."

"Is this about trust?"

Was it? Maybe.

"Let me stop you right there and explain the phone call, before things get taken out of hand." A grin pushed up the corners of his mouth, showing the hint of a dimple. "I trust you. I've let you in my house, and where I may have been a little hesitant about seeing us grow, I've mostly let you into my heart. And after all Jenna did to me, that's a start. A huge start." He sighed and cast his gaze down. "But I'm holding something back."

As his shoulders rolled in, my heart ached.

"Jenna left and moved back to the city. Remember when I mentioned how she got what she wanted and left?"

I nodded, reflecting on the conversation in the diner. Something about her parents not liking him, and constantly asking if they were pregnant. My eyes widened at the thought, and I searched out Jesse's. I didn't want to presume a thing, so I waited.

"When Jenna left, she was pregnant. She was ten weeks along when she moved into her parent's basement, and she hadn't yet told me. But her parents sure knew." A lacing of vitriol weaved through his words. He shook his head. "She didn't tell me until after her ultrasound when she found out the sex of our child. I wasn't even there when she gave birth."

I couldn't imagine having a child I couldn't see all the time. The constant heartache that would cause would be unmeasurable. And I also couldn't imagine taking the child away and not having a family. If I had gotten pregnant with Charlie's baby, he'd know. At least I'd like to think I'd tell him.

"What do you have?"

A twinkle returned to light up his eyes. "A daughter, Sarah. She's eighteen months old and quite the chatty little one. Looks just like her mother. That's who I was talking too."

He pulled out his phone and when it faced me, there was a little cherub of a face with dark eyes and hair. I saw Jesse in her features, but then again, I had no idea what Jenna looked like.

"She's cute, but I think she looks like you."

He stared at his phone. "You think so?" It deepened the smile.

"I do."

"That night when I came across you on the highway, I was just coming home from seeing her. Jenna and I agreed she's too young to spend the weekend away, so I go to her."

I nodded, an intense dislike of his ex-wife forming in my gut. She maybe got all she wanted, but clearly, not ethically. "How often do you see Sarah?"

He stared at the picture before turning it off and pocketing it. "Not as often as I'd like, that's for sure. But one weekend a month, I stay with friends and spend as much time with her. And I facetime Sarah all the time."

"That's great."

He squeezed my hand. "I'm sorry I kept it from you. But how do you tell someone you have a child that doesn't live with you? Even people around here don't know."

"I completely understand. Really, I get it." And I did.

Already, because of his job, he was a bit of an odd duck, and to think he has a child with the wife who hated this town. As I rolled the situation around in my head, his financial situation became even more clear. He likely paid a hefty parental support, which ate up his income, even though he didn't get to be a full-time father. Sometimes the system wasn't right.

"What about a job there?"

"I've thought about that, several times over. But the cost of living is much higher than here since this place is paid off. If I sold it, it still wouldn't be enough to get a decent down payment on a place there. Even an apartment would eat away my income."

Jenna really screwed him over and my heart went out to him.

134

There had to be other options, however, I was sure Jesse had thought them all through.

"Well, someday when she's older, I hope she'll be here for the holidays, and you can do all the fun things with her that we did together."

"That's the dream."

"It'll happen." I believed it and walked over to park myself between his legs when he turned to face me. My heart beat ultra fast as I hovered over him. Seeing the sadness on his face broke me a little, and I wanted to see that sweet smile and know I was responsible for putting it there. "I'm sorry things between you and Jenna didn't work out." I leaned my forearms on his strong shoulders. "But she lost out. Big time." My fingertips swirled on the back of his neck and I inhaled his fresh scent. "However, you're all mine to claim." I brushed my lips over his, taunting and teasingly.

His mouth parted and I dove in, exploring and tasting, all the while giving my heart to this wonderful man. As his hands gripped tighter around my waist, I wanted more. More of Jesse. More of his kiss. I wanted to explore everything he'd give me. And it was something I could do. All my life, I'd never taken chances – on anything. But this?

"I need you, Jesse."

"I need you too."

The sweetest words I'd ever heard. How wonderful it felt to be needed.

"I know it sounds crazy and risky, like wildly unsettled, but I've never been so sure of something in my life." And that truth set me free. Suddenly my future didn't seem so dismal and grey, picturing Jesse in it gave it life and colour.

He stared into the depths of my eyes. "What becomes of us now? What happens after the wedding?"

My shoulders lifted in defeat, but I couldn't stop the blossoming smile from spreading across my face. "I honestly don't know, but we'll find a way to make it work. Maybe I find a job here." I tapped the paper for good measure.

"Maybe I do make the move to the city." It wasn't said though with the best of intentions. More like a last resort.

I cupped his face and straddled his thighs. "I believe in us, of what's growing between us, more than I've believed in much of anything lately."

"Even with all my baggage?"

I laughed. "My luggage is way bigger than yours and if you can so easily accept me with mine, yours will be a walk in the park."

"So, we're really going to do this?" His eyes sparkled like a kid in the candy store, all lit up with endless possibilities.

"I'm in, if you are." I snuggled closer to him ensuring not a gap of air separated us.

"I'm all in." A smile cracked his whiskery face. "Merry Christmas, Mona."

My gaze danced between his eyes. "Merry Christmas. This

has been the best one ever."

I leaned forward and delicately touched my lips to his while cupping his perfect face and inhaling his sultry scent. I tipped my head and the moment his lips claimed mine, my body surrendered to his touch, knowing it was safe within his arms.

Mom's final written words lit up like a neon sign. This is what she wanted for me. This is what I never had with Charlie. Never once. My heart knew what was important. It knew *who* was important.

.

Chapter Sixteen

The sun caressed the sea as Lily and Eric kissed on the shoreline, their wedding ceremony ended, and the flash from the photographer's camera lighting their ecstatic faces. A million-dollar glow, if ever there was one, radiated out of each of them as the sun lowered itself into slumber.

Lily and Eric walked up the beach to the sound of crashing waves, between the rows of chairs to their back deck where they signed the papers, with Beth and Mitch as witnesses.

As the chairs emptied, Jesse and I walked hand-in-hand toward the house, stopping beside the lone giant oak tree on the beach for a kiss.

"You look absolutely stunning. It's not fair to your sister." Jesse trailed a finger down the side of my face, electrifying me with his delicate touch.

"And look at you." He'd really outdid himself dressed in a suit and tie in monochromatic colours, with his hair neatly styled. It upped his game, even if he was already a dashing man in jeans and a tee sporting a ball cap. "Care to dance?"

Wireless speakers had been placed on the decks of my old summer home and Eric's, and a current, sappy ballad was playing.

"Don't mind if I do." My fingers linked with Jesse's and we moved in time to the beat, the back of my wrap dress brushing against the sand as Jesse dipped me at the end, after which he planted a powerful kiss upon my needy lips.

"You know, we didn't even unwrap presents this morning." He righted me but held tight, which was fine by me. I didn't want to leave his side. It had been hard to leave this morning to go help Lily prepare.

I stood on the balls of my flats and placed my hands behind his head. "You can unwrap me later."

There was so much more of myself I was ready to give this man, to let him into the depths of my heart and soul. Years ago, when Charlie and I were fresh, things hadn't felt like this. However, between Jesse and me, there was a palpable electricity, a connection that felt natural and right on more levels than I'd ever thought possible. It was like two halves finding a perfect fit. And it all happened because I made the journey to Cheshire Bay, and my tire had blown along the way.

This fabulous man holding me close was everything I ever dreamed I wanted but thought I'd never find.

His kiss had the power to lift me and release my burdens, for he never judged me over it. Maybe if I had run into Jesse years ago, my life would've been different. But, maybe meeting him now had been the point.

I rested my head against him. "You're truly amazing."

"And you aren't? When I think back to that day on the highway... I was even running late that evening. Normally, I would've been home or at least pulling into the front of the house. But there I was, running behind, and I saw the blown tire on the road. And you..." He chuckled and ran his hand down my back.

His voice drifted off. "You were so interested in watching and learning how to change a tire. That hooked me because I'd never seen the likes of it."

"And you? You were so patient. Char- he would've ... well, it doesn't matter because you're here now and he's not." I planted a kiss on Jesse's lips.

Yes, my ex was long gone. Time to live in the present.

Jesse ran a finger down the side of my face again. It was a loving touch, and I turned my cheek into it fully.

He cleared his throat. "Come on. I think we should mingle, and I see some people you should probably be introduced to, since they are good friends of Eric's, your brother-in-law now."

I liked the sound of that. A brother-in-law. It meant the family was growing again.

Hand in hand, we made our way over to the gathering of people around Eric's porch. Only a few were recognizable, but the ones at my old summer home, none of those people were placeable.

Cedar was on Eric's porch, bouncing her baby girl in her arms. "That was a beautiful wedding. And that sunset, wow. I can't wait to see how their pictures turned out. Might be a great idea for my ceremony."

"When are you getting married?" I asked Cedar, smiling at the sleeping baby.

"No plans yet. It took us five years to get engaged, so it might be a while." She laughed, but it wasn't laced in malice, just a good-natured giggle.

Jesse squeezed my hand, and I watched him gaze softly upon the sleeping child. So many of those moments had been stolen from him.

"How's Saffron doing?"

Many a time, I'd heard new parents spend hours staring at a sleeping baby, and seeing Saffron curled up in Cedar's arms, I finally understood why. They were so peaceful and sweet.

"Growing like a weed. So is Ziggy. All they do is eat and sleep."

"As a baby should." I gently rubbed Saffron's head. It was so soft, and her hair was so fine. "Is she a good baby?"

"I'd say so. However, I'd appreciate more than a couple hours of sleep at a time. Maybe when they're older." Cedar scanned the area as a baby wail pierced the air.

Mitch appeared on the deck in moments with a screaming

child. "Zig's hungry again."

"As always. I'm a lean, mean, milking machine." She laughed and effortlessly took Ziggy from Mitch's arms, while still balancing Saffron. Had to admire her skill. "Excuse me."

Mitch stood there cradling his daughter. "So, do you have plans to return to the area? I know coming back was hard."

I didn't know Mitch at all, and small talk was a monumental task, however… "I do, actually, maybe soon. Seeing the Bay area as an adult, it's quite different than it was when I was a teen. I'd never attended a festival here before." I leaned against Jesse. It had all been because of him too.

A bubbly brunette with curly hair hopped onto the deck.

"Hey, Amber." Jesse walked over and gave her a hug.

"Hey, Jesse. Haven't seen you around much. How's life treating you?" Amber looked somewhat familiar, and I must've to her as well since she stopped and stared at me. "Holy smokes, how are you doing, Mona?"

"Oh my god, hi." That's why she rang a bell. Amber and I used to hang out back when we were teens. Sort of. If you could call it that.

"You know each other?" Jesse bounced his focus between us.

"Amber knew all the cool spots Lily could be hanging out at."

"Were you one of her keepers as well?" Jesse asked Amber with a light-hearted laugh.

She grinned. "Oh, god, not at all. I just had my eye and ear on the pulse of the town. Knew what was going on, who what and where kind of thing."

"And how are things going for you now?" I was genuinely intrigued since it had been years.

She hesitated and shifted on her feet. "Great. Eric had a beautiful wedding and I'm thrilled for them. He deserves all the happiness in the world. Lily has changed and settled down and that makes him happy, which makes me happy."

Lily and Amber never really did get along. Lily had mentioned Amber was more a friend to Eric, and best friends with Cedar.

"How are things with you? Are you two together?" She stared at our joined hands.

Jesse spoke first. "Yes. But it's brand new."

"We all have to start somewhere, right? Speaking of which, there he is." She waved and a tall, gorgeous guy waltzed over. "This is my fiancé, Antonio."

We all shook hands.

"He flew over from Greece yesterday." There was a wink at the end of her sentence.

"Sheshire Bay is beautiful." He had a thick accent too. "As was wedding. Gorgeous." He faced his fiancée. "Ember, we should plan beach ceremony."

"Oh, I'm totally on board with that." She looked at all of us and nodded.

It was hard to not agree. The ceremony had truly been magical and put a nice spin on Christmas. The holiday now had a different look to it. It was no longer filled with dread and a sense of sadness, instead, as I gazed around the beach bathed in the darkening colours of twilight and bonfires, and spotted endless couples and families, it meant happiness and chance to start fresh.

Everyone was entitled to a do over once in their lives. Lily had hers when she moved back to Cheshire Bay and maybe with the reconciliation, the red box finally unwrapped, and Jesse, I believed with my whole heart, this was my do-over.

I cupped the side of his face. "Merry Christmas, Jesse Lancaster."

The broadest grin I'd ever seen stretched from ear to ear. "Merry Christmas, Mona Baker."

Epilogue

Two years later…
Christmas Eve

I tapped my ear for the incoming call and shifted my bag between hands as I tugged my keys out of my purse. "Hey."

"Are you still at work?"

"No," but I giggled as I said it, so he knew I was lying. "I'm just locking up."

Which was the truth. My key twisted in the lock of Lancaster Baker, an accounting firm. A small beans accounting firm in the town of Cheshire Bay, my new home.

Twenty-two months ago, I made a decision and decided to stop travelling across the island to see Jesse. Rather, I moved in with him, and funneled the monthly savings – since there was no mortgage payment – into opening my own business. While not a roaring success, I did have to hire another to help me out.

"She's landing in five minutes." Was he pacing back and forth at the airport?

"I know. Sorry, I got stuck on a project, but I'm heading home right now." It never got old. *Home.*

"We'll be there in about thirty minutes." Jesse's voice was upbeat and ecstatic.

"And I'll have everything ready. Promise." The lock slid into place, and I walked over to the truck since Jesse had driven my car.

"Merry Christmas, Mona." The owner of the reality shop beside me was just closing up his office.

"Merry Christmas, Stan."

I drove home, down the lane full of homes fully decorated in twinkling lights and blow-up snowmen and an igloo made from plastic, since the bay area hadn't received much snow yet. Our house was the Griswold's of houses, and I finally understood what that statement meant as I had a hand in making sure there were more than enough lights to make this side of the island visible from the sea.

Parking the truck, I dashed into the house and double checked everything was good to go.

Sarah's room was perfect. A little girl bed with pink sheets and unicorns was ready for its first Christmas guest; the first time Sarah was allowed to spend the holiday with her father. It took some convincing, and a small threat to take her to court, but Jesse and I had Sarah for the holidays.

I folded and refolded the bed to make it just perfect, and

double checked under the tree for her pile of gifts. The coolest present, one Sarah wouldn't know about until her eighteenth birthday, was a giant clear globe hanging near the back of the tree. Every visit with Sarah, Jesse would scratch out a memory or two, or three, and scroll it up to add to the globe. He's loved that idea ever since I unwrapped Mom's final gift. One of the gifts I've wrapped for him is a package of archival quality paper, so the paper will outlast the memories.

A final check of everything, and I waited as Jesse brought Sarah home. All the lights were on, even though it was still broad daylight out. Who cared? It was Christmas Eve.

The car approached and my stomach bubbled with delight. Her first overnight in his place, after three and a half years.

Jesse parked and ran over to unbuckle Sarah while Jenna and her fiancé exited the car.

I hopped down the stairs and sidewalk to meet them, wrapping them in a hug.

"Hi guys."

"Hey, Mona." Jenna's fiancé, Jim, was a stand-up guy and when we'd get together in their city, we always had dinner with them, and he always made us feel welcome and part of the family.

Jenna was a little put off about being here, and it was easy to see. Her lips curled in mild disgust as she scanned the area – her old home. However, she refused to let Jesse fly Sarah over alone or even with him, so she packed her own bag for a few days.

"While Jesse gets Sarah settled, I'll take you over to the B&B." I grabbed one of the suitcases from the trunk.

Sarah bounded over to me and wrapped my leg in a hug. I set down the luggage and lifted her into my arms.

"Hi, Mommy Mo." Her sweet nickname for me.

I gave her a squeeze and tickled her nose. "Hello, my sweet. Are you ready for a fun few days?"

She nodded in excitement, nearly colliding with my face.

I set her down and picked up the suitcase again. "First, I'm going to take your mommy and daddy Jim over to their house, okay? And when I come back, we're going to have all the fun."

Sarah hugged Jim and her mom, who had a hard time letting go, something I could understand. The first Christmas without your child would be tough, but Jesse's had to do it for three years.

However…

"C'mon." I tipped my head toward the house at the end of the lane. "Lily's got your place ready to go. You're going to love it."

Jim grabbed the rest of the bags as Jenna finally stood up, tears in her eyes. "See you soon, honey. Mommy loves you."

I threw my gaze to Jesse and tipped my head in a questioning gaze.

Jesse cleared his throat. "Being that it's Christmas and all, we're having a big family dinner tomorrow on the back decks. We'd love it if you joined us."

My heart swelled at the olive branch extension. Jenna hadn't offered up any time last Christmas, but okayed him to see Sarah on Christmas Eve, for a few hours.

Jenna leaned against Jim as tears streamed down her cheeks. "I'd," she gazed up at Jim. "We'd very much like that."

"Great." Jesse took Sarah's hand and led her towards the house. "Dinner's at four. Just come on out. You won't miss it."

It would be impossible to miss with the giant bonfire and the party goers.

He hunched down to Sarah's height. "Want to see your room?"

"So, the place you're staying at used to be my old beach house, and it's now a B&B run by my sister…" I led them down the lane, past Dakota's house, past Eric and Lily's and their family of four, and over to the steps of my old home.

I had so many memories, the best was the most recent one. Because the furnace was busted and the home ice cold, I stayed with Jesse. That stay changed my life. It gave me a new family with Eric and his friends, and it gave me Jesse. Over the past couple years, it also gave me more with a stepdaughter and her family. It made me believe in myself, and the magic of Christmas.

More Fabulous Reads

For the most up-to-date listings, please check the website:
www.hmshander.com

Dear Reader

Thank you so much for taking the time to read Christmas in Cheshire Bay. I'd felt my time in Cheshire Bay had come to an end, but then a boxed set contribution called out to me, asking for a short story – novella Christmas themed story. YES! I could write a Christmas story, and that's how the Christmas in Cheshire Bay came to be. I couldn't wait to have the whole gang back together to celebrate Lily's wedding and to wrap back to the first story. I seriously loved writing this one, and many times I ugly cried on Mona's behalf.

However this story is finished, I know deep in my heart I am not even close to being finished with my time in Cheshire Bay. There are at least four more stories coming, perhaps all ending with a New Year's in Cheshire Bay. I can't wait to finish them and start leaking out the first details.

Would you like to be the first to know of upcoming releases, see the covers before anyone else, and just have all the insider information? Then you'll want to join my twice-a-month mailing list. Connect through my website – www.hmshander.com. I promise not to spam you, and I keep things fun with freebies and a scavenger hunt. Your time is valuable, and I appreciate how you've spent time reading my story (thank you for that!).

Finally, if you don't mind, I'd love a review on your favourite retailer site for each of the novellas you've read. It doesn't have to be long, even just as simple as "Eric/Mitch/Antonio/Jesse are my new book boyfriends" works. Reviews and ratings help me gain visibility, and as I'm sure you can tell, reviews are tough to come by. Thank you so much for spending time with me.

Yours,

H.M. Shander

acknowledgements

If one good thing came out of the pandemic in 2020, it was these books – I'm absolutely in love with this series and all the characters. They are each unique, but together, they form a beautiful series, if I do say so myself.

I'm in awe of being able to do what I love, and to fulfill my dream, but writing these thanks yous never gets easier. Never. Always afraid I'll miss someone, or a category will be left out. And then I wonder, does anyone even read these? I know as an author, I do, but I wonder if readers do? Anyways, writing a book for the most part, is a solo endeavor, but I could not have this ready for you to read if not for the cheerleading and support of some magnificent people in my life.

First – my Shander family, whom you may know on my social media platforms as Hubs, The Teen, and Little Dude. Thank you from the bottom of my heart for letting me pursue what I love doing, for something that allows me to transport myself to another time and place – the summer of 2020 was a particular straining time, and you gave me this golden escape into the pages. For that, I'll be forever grateful, and if this series does well, we're going to do something incredible. Like really big and fun. Thank you for cheerleading as I had a sale, and watching the numbers climb. Thank you for encouraging me to keep going and to chase my dreams, and for the nonstop coffees I sometimes needed when I was on a role. I love you all with my whole heart.

To my parents and in-laws and extended family – Thank you for your support, and encouraging your friends and family to give my books a try. Having you visit me at markets and book signings means the world. I have an amazing family, and every day I'm thankful to you all. Thanks for being you.

To my wonderfully dedicated alpha reader – Mandy. My

trusted go-to writing pal, the one who reads the first cleaned up draft. Where would I be without your support and guidance? Probably still cowering in a corner. Your comments and feedback are vital to me. I never have to wait long, and before I know it, my inbox has a response, and 99% of the time, your advice is bang on. I'm so glad we're in this business together, and you know I'm your biggest fan and cheerleader! You're going to go big, and I'm tagging along on the ride. You deserve the very best.

To my critique partner – Josephine. Thank you for spending your free time reading my words and pointing out what didn't make sense and what needed to be expanded on. How many times did I redo that opening chapter in Return? LOL, and Awake? You had your work cut out with that, eh? But, as always, your insight was invaluable, and the stories are better with your touch! Thank you.

To my beta readers – Shauna, Melissa, and Dawn. Thank you for cheering for the good, highlighting the bad, and letting me know what worked and what needed more explanation. Your feedback and insight are a gift I cherish.

To my cover designer – Eleanor. Great job! I'm super thrilled with how well all the covers turned out, including the special edition print cover! I simple adore all of them and can't stop staring! I'm so blessed to have discovered your talents, and I look forward to many more covers designed by you.

To my editor – Irina. Thanks for your dedication to fixing my errors and highlighting the inconsistencies. I think I'm getting better, right? At least it's not the same corrections every time. Heh-heh.

If I missed you, it certainly wasn't intentional. I know I couldn't be where I am without the help of so many others. Thank you! And thank you for reading and making it all the way to the end. You all rock.

about the author

USA TODAY bestselling author H.M. Shander is a star-gazing, romantic at heart who once attended Space Camp and wanted to pilot the space shuttle, not just any STS – specifically Columbia. However, the only shuttle she operates in her real world is the #momtaxi; a reliable electric car that transports her two kids to school and various sporting events. When she's not commandeering Elektra, you can find the elementary school librarian surrounded by classes of children as she reads the best storybooks in multiple voices. After she's tucked her endearing kids into bed and kissed her trophy husband goodnight, she moonlights as a contemporary romance novelist; the writer of sassy heroines and sweet, swoon-worthy heroes who find love in the darkest of places.

If you want to know when her next heart-filled journey is coming out, you can follow her on Twitter (@HM_Shander), Facebook (hmshander), or check out her website at www.hmshander.com.

Thanks for reading– all the way to the very end.

Manufactured by Amazon.ca
Bolton, ON

36208297R00090